ELIZABETH LAIRD

The PRINCE WHO WALKED WITH LIONS

MACMILLAN CHILDREN'S BOOKS

First published 2012 by Macmillan Children's Books

This edition published 2012 by Macmillan Children's Books
a division of Macmillan Publishers Limited
20 New Wharf Road, London N1 9RR
Basingstoke and Oxford
Associated companies throughout the world
www.panmacmillan.com

ISBN 978-0-330-53039-2

1 3 5 7 9 8 6 4 2

A CIP catalogue record for this book is available from
the British Library.

Printed and bound by CPI Group (UK) Ltd, Croydon CR0 4YY

For Michael and Patsy Sargent

Before you start reading . . .

History books are usually written long after events are over and the people who lived through them have died. Historians can never know everything about the past, especially what was in people's hearts. It's their job to relate the facts as accurately as they can. Novelists have a different job to do. We try to help our readers understand how it felt to be involved in the events of the past, and why people behaved in the way they did.

A few facts to get you started:

Abyssinia is the old name for the African country we now call Ethiopia.

Prince Alamayu, his father the Emperor Theodore and his mother Queen Tirunesh were real people, and so were General Napier, Captain Speedy, Mr Rassam and many of the other characters who took part in the Abyssinia Campaign in 1868. Most of this story is based on accounts of what happened by people who were there. The Cotton family on the Isle of Wight and Dr Jex-Blake of Rugby School were real people too, but Alamayu's school friends are imagined.

A *shamma* is a heavy white cloth, like a thick shawl, which all Abyssinians, men and women, wore wrapped around their shoulders, as Ethiopians still do today.

Tej is an alcoholic drink made out of honey.

The correct spelling for Prince Alamayu's name is 'Alemayehu', but I have kept the simpler spelling which he used himself when he signed his name.

Elizabeth Laird

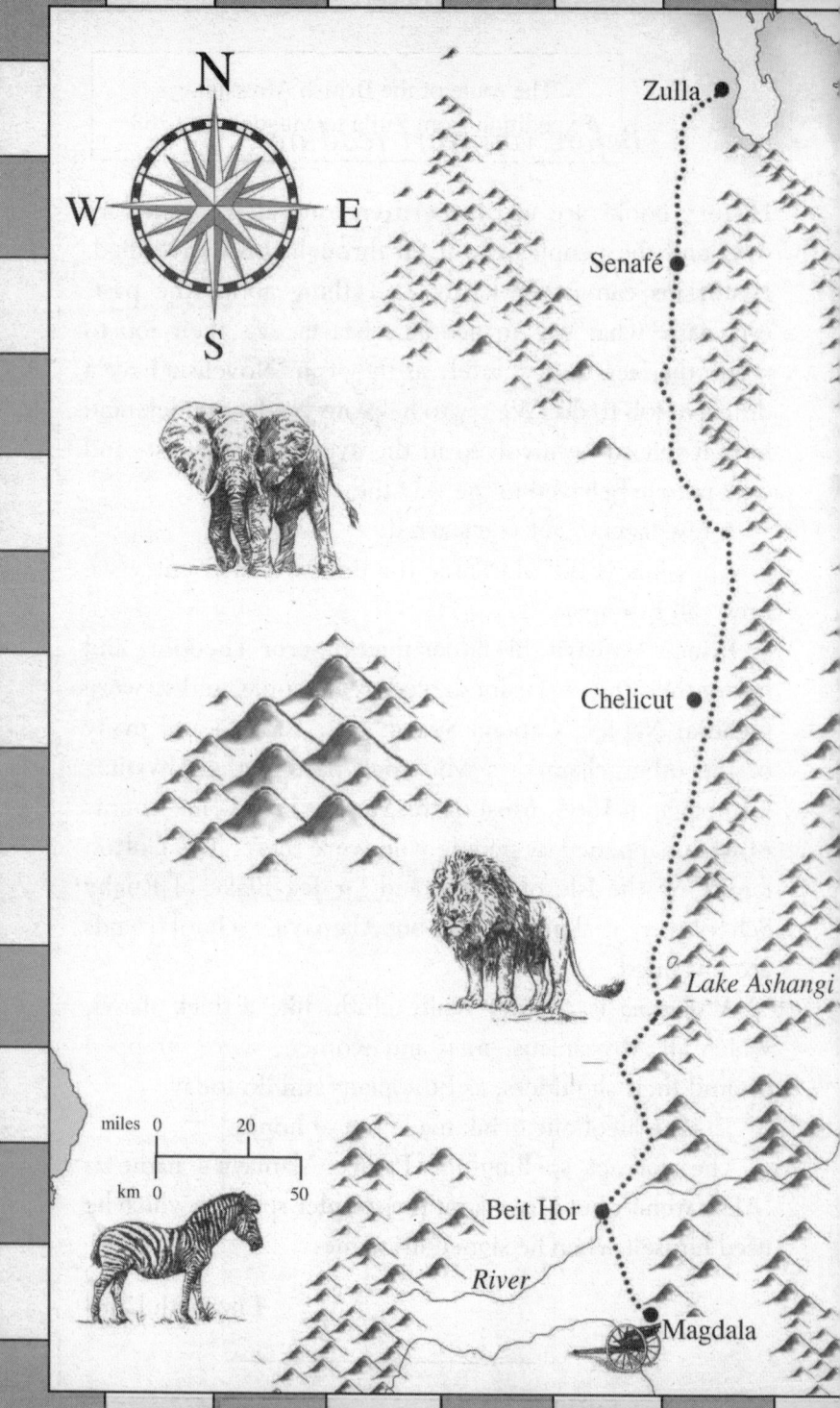

The route of the British Abyssinian
Expedition from Zulla to Magdala in 1868

RED SEA

Alexandria
Suez

Abyssinia

AFRICA

Dejas Alamayoo
1st May 1868.

S n of the Emperor Theodoro

Sketched at Dilder in Abyssinia

Prince Alamayu of Abyssinia as a child

The walls of this room have been whitewashed. Light streams in through the windows and hurts my eyes. It's not very bad in the mornings, when my mind is hazy and I only want to rest. But in the afternoon the fever takes hold and the white walls seem to bulge as if there were crowds of people behind them, trying to push their way through.

The worst time is the evening. Nurse Thomson comes in and stands over me with a glass full of an evil-tasting medicine. I can't clearly make her out. She seems to be someone else entirely. Instead of her round face with the white cap and its flying ribbons sitting on top, I see the brown skin and flashing black eyes of my father, or the flaming red hair and brilliant blue eyes of Captain Speedy, or even the plump pink cheeks of Queen Victoria.

'Who is this boy?' they seem to say.

'Don't you know me?' I try to say. 'I'm Alamayu.'

They shake their heads at me.

'You don't belong here, Alamayu. You ought to be at home.'

'I know!' My voice is dry and croaking. 'Where? Where's home? Where?'

'Shh, dear,' Nurse Thomson says, pressing me down on to the pillow again and putting the glass to my lips. 'Drink this.'

The medicine's strong and at last it makes me go to sleep, but only after it's filled me full of dreams. Not dreams, exactly. Memories. I thought I'd forgotten everything that happened to me when I was a child, a prince, in Abyssinia. I've spent the last years trying to become an English boy like all the others here at Rugby School. Those old days and all those far-off things – the lions padding around outside my father's house, the eagles circling over the mountain tops, the bright African sun glinting on our spears and muskets and on the enemy's helmets and rifles – have been locked away for so long that I thought they were gone forever.

It seems that I hadn't forgotten after all. Every evening the bulging walls seem to burst open and I can see myself, a young boy, back at home with Amma, my mother, upstairs in the King's House in Magdala. It's as if everything that happened to me then is happening again. Part of me is inside that little prince, being him again. Part of me is my new, older self, watching him.

My father was a king. More than that, he was a king of kings. An emperor. And he loved me.

'My boy,' he called me. 'My prince.'

When he wasn't away at war he would send a slave to the house my mother and I shared with the other women. The man would come to the gate of our compound, and one of our own slaves would run silently up our house's outer staircase and cough politely outside the door to the upper rooms.

'Who is it? What do you want?' Amma's old servant Abebech would screech, dropping the comb she was using on my mother's hair.

'His Majesty calls for the Prince, his son,' the slave would say in a respectful murmur.

'It's me! Father wants me!' I would shout, and I'd rush to the doorway.

Abebech was always too quick for me. She would shoot out one long skinny arm and catch me in a tight grip, and my mother would say, in her soft tired voice, 'Wait, Alamayu, straighten your tunic. Come here. Look, your face is dirty.'

'Father doesn't care.'

I would be dancing with impatience, trying to wriggle out of Abebech's grasp. I would do it too. I'd be out through the door and tumbling down the stairs, racing across the compound to the gate, then the slave would take my hand and I'd trot beside him to the royal enclosure.

I was seven years old then. I didn't know anything about the world beyond our Abyssinian mountains. The sounds I heard were the whoop of hyenas in the night, the chanting of priests in the stillness of dawn, the trample of horses' hoofs, the shouts of men, the crackle of musket fire, the clatter of spears, the screams of the wounded and the croaking of vultures. The smells I knew were the smoke of our fires, the spices of our rich cooking, the incense that scented my mother's house, and my father's sweat, when he picked me up and I buried my face in his chest. I had never heard of the British, or of Queen Victoria, or railways.

Last night as I lay in this bed, in the sickroom here in Rugby School, the fever took hold of me strongly. The white walls and ceiling faded away and I could see my first home as clearly as if I was standing right there in front of it.

We lived in my father's capital. In Europe it would have been thought of as a village, a simple collection of huts and houses, but it was on the summit of Magdala, a dizzyingly high flat-topped mountain. Our house, the King's House, was the biggest

Magdala

building, bigger even than the church. In my feverish dream I climbed the steep path from Selamge, the flat plain on the shoulder of the mountain, and scrambled up the rough stony path to the outer gates. My father held me gently by the hand, and when the sentries saw us coming they put down their spears and leaped to open the wooden doors, bowing low as we passed.

The side of the mountain of Magdala rose in a sheer wall of stone on our right. On our left a cliff plunged down from the narrow path. And when I remember this, the nightmare begins. My father's grip shifts from my hand to my wrist. His eyes, which are usually soft and full of love when he looks at me, harden until they are twin black stones. His dark skin flushes a deeper brown. His thin lips are pulled back from his teeth. I can even smell the stench of death rising from the corpses that lie rotting at the foot of the cliff.

I am seized with panic. Will he cut off my hands and feet then throw me down to my death, as he did to hundreds of his enemies? As I stand, unable to move, my father picks me up in his strong arms. His eyes soften. His painful grip becomes a loving embrace. He holds me to his chest and as I draw in my breath to sob he strokes my hair and murmurs in my ear, 'You are a prince of Abyssinia. Never let them see you cry.'

I fling my arms round his neck and swallow my tears, and for a moment all comfort, all safety and all love are there.

Then, as we stand on the perilous path, the ground beneath my father's feet starts to crumble, and there's a roar as the cliff gives way. He can't hold me any more.

'Alamayu!' I hear him call, and then I'm falling, falling, all alone.

The memory dream ends there. I land back in my bed in the cold middle of this cold island of England. The fever has gone, the night light has burned out and the night nurse is asleep and snoring in the armchair, with the grey light of dawn creeping in through the crack between the curtains.

The clock on the school tower chimes six.

'Magdala!' I whisper to myself.

I lie with my eyes shut, trying to transport myself back there again. I know that if only I can reach the top of the path and pass through the inner gates, I can run out on to the broad flat top of the mountain to the gate opening in the fence that surrounds our compound. Smoke from the cooking fires will be steaming out through the thatch of the kitchen huts behind the main house. In our upper room, the Queen, my mother, will be sitting cross-legged on her silk cushions with her favourite book, *The Life of the Virgin Mary*, open on its little wooden stand in front of her. Her lips will be moving soundlessly as she reads. She'll reach forward to turn the heavy parchment page, but then she'll see me, and her arched brows will rise, and she'll open her arms, and I'll run into . . .

I am so nearly there. I so nearly reach her. But however close I try to come, I can't see Amma's face.

So here I lie, and the memory dream has faded, and the long day stretches ahead. If today is anything like yesterday and the day before, I'll drift in and out of sleep this morning, and then, towards evening, the fever will climb again and bring the dream memories back. I half long for them and half dread them.

At least I have something to look forward to today. My friend Beetle (his real name is John Forster) is coming to visit me. They won't let him stay long in case he tires me out, but it will be good just to see him and know that he's bothered to come. My other good friend Bull (his real name is Samuel Bulliver) has asked to come too, but they won't let him. I don't mind much. Bull is so big and restless and talks so loudly that he really would wear me out. It makes me tired just to think about him.

I suppose that Beetle's my friend because he's an outsider at Rugby, rather like me. It's not that he's a foreigner too, or dark-skinned, as I am. It's just that he's – different.

Beetle doesn't seem to notice what other people think. He doesn't seem to care about who's popular and who isn't. He doesn't try to make people like him. He is not really interested in cricket or football. (The football we invented at this school, which other people call 'rugby football', is just called 'football' here). It's all one to Beetle if our house (Elsee's) doesn't win a match. He stares at me through his thick round glasses if I try to explain to him how much I want to score a try.

Beetle likes insects and nature generally.

'Insects are a lot like people, if you think about it,' he says. 'They've all got their special ways of doing things.'

I don't understand what Beetle means exactly because I don't know anything about insects, but he certainly understands a lot about people too, more than many of the boys, anyway. He sees more about what goes on in school than I do.

The best thing about being friends with Beetle is that he has always accepted me the way I am. He's never been nosy. He sticks up for me too, in his odd way. He doesn't pester me to tell him about the Abyssinia Campaign. He doesn't say, like some of the other boys do, 'Your father was that darkie madman who thought he could fight the British, and win.'

You could say that Beetle's eccentric. That's what I think, anyway. The other fellows say he's a crank. A rum cove. Crazy as a bedbug. They laugh at the way his collar sticks up.

Beetle is no better at Latin and learning by heart and writing stupid essays than I am. I sit next to him in our form room. I don't think he tries very hard to learn, especially when he's bored. I do try, sometimes anyway, but my mind goes dreaming away. Then the thought jumps into my head that a prince of Abyssinia shouldn't have to learn Latin verbs and all that mumbo-jumbo like a low-born priest, and after that I can't take in anything at all.

This morning, the groundsmen, working outside below the window of the sickbay, have made a bonfire of the leaves that have been spinning down off the trees for the last couple of weeks. Tiny wafts of smoke have crept in round the loose-fitting window, and the smell has taken me right back to Abyssinia, to Mr Rassam's house, where a fire almost always burned on a hearthstone in the middle of the room.

Mr Rassam was the British envoy and one of my father's European prisoners. I didn't know most of them, though I can dimly see, in my mind's eye, their pale figures shuffling about our flat mountain top and hear the chains clanking around their ankles. Most of the time they were kept closely guarded in their prison huts. (There were hundreds of Abyssinian prisoners too, but their prison was on a different part of the mountain top, and they were never allowed outside.)

People often ask me why my father imprisoned most of the Europeans who came to Abyssinia. I don't really know the answer.

'They insulted him,' I say, and try to change the subject.

It was true, after all. My father, a king of kings, wanted more than anything else to make friends with Europeans. He wanted them to teach him to make guns, so that he could defeat his enemies. But the British never bothered to answer his courteous letters. They probably put them into a drawer and forgot about them. I know that some of the travellers and missionaries who came to Abyssinia irritated Father. I'm not sure why. I think he thought they were spies. In the end he locked them all up to stop them making more trouble. I don't think he ever thought that the British would send a huge army to rescue such a small group of people. There were only twenty or thirty foreigners in his prisons, after all.

Being the British envoy, Mr Rassam was the most important of the European prisoners and he was allowed more freedom than the others. He had his round thatched hut, and his own servant, Samuel, was allowed to stay with him and look after him. He even had a little garden outside, where he liked to grow vegetables. My father liked Mr Rassam, even though he had taken him prisoner, because he was more respectful than the others. They often used to talk together.

I liked Mr Rassam too. He used to sit on a stool beside his fire, the smoke wafting about the house, holding his hands out to warm them when the evenings were cold.

'Well, little Prince,' he would say (he could speak my language well, unlike the others), 'and have you shot any birds today with that catapult of yours?'

Then he would teach me to say things in English.

Sometimes he would just sit there and sigh and look down into the fire. He was sad, I suppose, to be a prisoner so far from home. I didn't understand that then. I do now.

If Father had let the European prisoners go, the British would never have sent an army to Magdala to rescue them. Their rifles wouldn't have torn our brave warriors to pieces, my father wouldn't have been defeated and I wouldn't be lying imprisoned here under these heavy blankets, too weak to move, coughing because of the woodsmoke and waiting for Beetle to come.

Sometimes, in this school full of men and boys, you can forget that such beings as women and girls actually exist. I don't mind. I prefer it to having too many of them close by. But I wish I could remember what my mother looked like. She's there sometimes in my dreams, but she always slips away from me before I'm fully awake.

She was beautiful. Captain Speedy told me that. She was small, light and very young. She was married to my father when she was only twelve years old, and she was thirteen when I was born, no older than I am now. She hardly ever smiled or laughed. I only remember her tears and her prayers, always long, long prayers. She used to pick me up and hold me so tightly that the pattern of the scarlet embroidery which ran in ribs down the front of her white dress would be imprinted on my cheek when she let me go.

I only twice saw my father and mother together. He never stayed in the King's House on the windy heights of Magdala. He was nearly always away, leading his armies into battle against his countless enemies. Even when he was at home he slept in a simple tent, preferring the hard life of a soldier.

Once he came into the room where I was playing in a corner with my string of ivory beads. Amma was reading as usual, rocking backwards and forwards, saying the Bible words soundlessly to herself. I know she heard someone come in. I know she realized it was him. But she didn't stand up, as she ought to have done for her husband and her king. She went on reading, only lifting her eyebrows a little in a look of pained contempt.

I saw the dark rage rise in my father's face. It brought the familiar surge of fear. I dropped my beads and crawled behind the cushion on which my mother was sitting. Father's lips were pressed so tightly together in his anger that a pale line had appeared around his mouth.

'Look at me, woman!' he commanded furiously. 'Get up! Do you think I am a servant?'

Behind him Gebre the eunuch, who slept across the doorway at night, was holding on to the doorpost with a trembling hand.

My mother looked up, rose slowly to her feet and shook out the folds of her dress.

'I didn't hear you enter,' she said coolly. 'I was talking to someone greater than you – the Lord of Kings Himself.'

She knew where to touch him. The wrath of God was the only thing that could frighten Father. A cautious, wary look came into his eyes as the anger died out of them. He didn't say another word, but turned on his heel. Then, by the door, he saw fat Yetemegnu, the one the British called his second queen. She wasn't a queen, not like Amma. She was just – just his woman. She was sitting in the shadows,

Reading the Bible in an Abyssinian house

her mirror fallen into her lap. She smiled up at him, her mouth half open in her loathsome way. He nodded curtly and she got up and trotted out after him, like an eager dog.

'What does Father want with *her?*' I asked Amma. How stupid I was then, not to understand.

'Don't ask me,' she snapped. 'She's nothing but a . . .' Then she sighed so deeply that the links of her gold necklace clattered on her chest. 'Go outside and play, Alamayu. Tell Abebech to bring me some oil for my head. It's aching so badly I can hardly see.'

Before I had reached the door she called me back.

'Don't forget,' she said wearily, 'that your royal blood comes from me. He –' she jerked her chin towards the rectangle of light in the doorway through which Father had just disappeared – 'He calls himself a king now, but he was once only a bandit, and his mother was a humble herb seller.'

I hated her saying that. I used to clap my hands over my ears whenever she spoke badly of my father. Anyway, I knew that she was wrong. I had often gone where she did not go, to stand beside my father when he reclined on his throne, his long hands resting on the shining silk that covered it, his face shaded from the sun by a silver embroidered umbrella, while a priest intoned in a sing-song voice the roll of my father's ancestors – *my* ancestors – back and back through the ages, name after name, until he came to King Solomon himself who married the Queen of Sheba, and Solomon's father David, and from him all the way back to the first man Adam and his wife Eve.

Once I blurted out to a group of boys here at school that I was descended from King Solomon. I'd hoped to make myself popular, but it went wrong.

'Lying, aren't we, darkie?' one of the boys said. 'King Solomon was in the Bible, so he must have been a white man. Everyone knows that.'

'He was a Jew,' I said. 'Like Our Lord himself.'

He seemed about to deny it, but then I saw him hesitate and he turned away, and the crowd around me dissolved. I learned after that to say nothing about myself if I could avoid it. I tried to forget everything I knew about my people and my country. I succeeded so well that I even forgot who I was, as well as all the things that had happened to me, until this fever came.

It was Amma, I think, who first made me realize that everything in my life was going to change. She saw that my father's habit of imprisoning all the Europeans who came to Abyssinia, forcing them to work for him and putting them in chains, would lead to disaster.

'Be polite to the *ferenjis*,' she would say to me. ('*Ferenji*' is our Abyssinian word for Europeans.) 'They're your father's prisoners now, but one day you're going to need them.'

My father was miles away from Magdala, fighting the rebels on the far side of Abyssinia, and while he was gone Amma was careful to be kind to Mr Rassam and the other European prisoners. She cooked dishes for them with her own hands and sent me off to deliver them.

I was doing this one day, and had gone past the guards and was nearly at the door of Mr Rassam's prison house, when I heard, from the voices and the clattering of chains inside, that some of the other *ferenji* prisoners were with him. They were speaking English of course. I stopped to listen. I liked to try to recognize the few words that Mr Rassam had taught me, but I couldn't understand much at all. After a few minutes I was bored, and just as I was about to cough politely to let them know I was there, Samuel, Mr Rassam's servant, ran past me into the house. He didn't even notice me.

'Sir!' he called out to Mr Rassam in Amharic (our language). 'They've landed! The British have landed! Thousands of men, with mules and horses and even elephants! They've come to rescue you!'

I wasn't really shocked that Samuel, who was an Abyssinian after all, sounded so happy. I knew that many of our own people didn't like Father. It was why his prisons were so full.

Mr Rassam gave a shout and started speaking English to the other men. They were cheering and clapping, as if they'd been freed already. I didn't know what to do. I felt too shy to go in, but I was afraid to go back to Amma with the bowl of chicken stew still in my hands.

The noise inside the hut quietened down as Mr Rassam asked Samuel, 'How long before they get here?'

'Weeks, sir. Months. You know what the terrain is like.

All the way across the desert first, and where will they find water for the men, let alone the mules and horses? And then – to climb up here! Up and down, over one mountain after another. It can't be done in a hurry. In fact, sir, I don't see how they can do it at all, with the heavy guns they're carrying.'

I heard a strange sound then and peered round the doorpost to look inside. Mr Rassam was laughing. It was a creaking sort of sound, as if he hadn't laughed for a long time and had forgotten how to do it.

'Oh, they'll do it,' he said. 'You don't know the British. They'll . . .'

He stopped and lowered his voice. I had to strain to hear what he said.

'Be careful, Samuel. We must all be careful. The King's spies are everywhere. You know how easily he falls into a rage. One careless word, one hint of disrespect, and we're all dead men. That goes for our servants too.'

I didn't like hearing him say that. I crept back to the compound gateway and put the dish of chicken stew into the hands of one of the men guarding it. Then I ran back home to my mother.

Amma was sitting on her cushions while Abebech plaited her hair.

'Did Mr Rassam like my stew?' she asked me, yawning and looking at herself in her mirror.

'I don't know. I gave it to one of the guards.'

She frowned and put the mirror down.

'Why? I told you to give it to him yourself.'

'There were other *ferenjis* with him, Amma. They were all talking. Samuel came running in. He said that the British are coming. They've landed. Who are the British, anyway? Is there chicken stew for our dinner? I'm hungry.'

She ignored me. She was looking across at Yetemegnu, who had dropped the hank of cotton she was spinning and had lumbered to her feet.

'It's going to happen, then,' Amma said quietly, and I was surprised because I'd never heard her speak to Yetemegnu before without shouting in a rage, although for months they had been forced to share the same house.

Yetemegnu said nothing. They stood, their eyes locked together.

'You must talk to the King,' Amma said, 'as soon as he returns to Magdala. He might listen to you. Tell him to let the prisoners go, or the British will come here and kill us all.'

Yetemegnu didn't answer for a long moment. I think she was as surprised as I was. She stood there, working her pudgy fingers in and out of the folds of her long white dress. At last she shrugged her shoulders. 'Theodore is a lion,' she said loudly, and I saw her eyes slide towards the two eunuchs standing at the doorway, then back to Amma's face. 'He will lay all his enemies in the dust at his feet and trample on them like the snakes they are.'

Amma's eyes too flickered towards the eunuchs.

'Of course,' she said flatly.

Yetemegnu sank down again on to her stool. Amma leaned back against her pillows.

'Amma, I told you, I'm hungry,' I said.

No one even looked at me. Something had shifted between my mother and her hated rival. It was as if they had become allies of a sort.

The door to the sickbay opened a little while ago. I lifted my head, hoping to see Beetle, but it was only Dr Bartlett. He held my wrist to take my pulse and tapped my chest.

'Not so much fever today?' he said to Nurse Thomson, who was standing to attention at the foot of my bed.

'No, sir. It doesn't usually go up until later in the day.'

'And the cough?'

'Bad, very bad, during the night.'

'Hmm.'

He had been looking grave, but saw my eyes on his face and smiled kindly.

'Try not to worry, young man. We'll get you on your feet again. Best not to think about getting back into school for the time being, eh? Let's take one day at a time.'

He and Nurse Thomson went over to the door and talked quietly. They thought I couldn't hear them, I suppose. I made out the words 'congestion of the lungs', and 'blood in the sputum'. Then they saw me looking at them and went out.

I *want* to think about getting back to school, whatever Dr Bartlett says. I don't mind being a schoolboy at Rugby now that I'm used to it, though I hated it at the beginning when I was new and everyone stared at me all the time. More than anything else I want to get back to playing football.

The best times here are the half-holidays, because Beetle and I go off across the meadows to hunt for insects and all sorts of other wild creatures. (At least, Beetle looks for them. I just tag along with him, glad to be out in the open where I can think my own thoughts.)

When he's out looking for things, Beetle becomes like one of the animals he loves to watch. He walks stealthily and is careful not to make a noise. I copy him. I'm lighter than he is, and I know how to be still and quiet. I learned that lesson a long, long time ago.

Beetle's eyes can pick up the smallest movement in the grass. He knows if a vole is cowering there. His ears catch the lightest splash when a water rat slides into the stream. He knows where the crayfish are. He can put his finger into one of their holes, and when the silly thing nips it, Beetle pulls it out.

I never really listen when Beetle goes on about finding a rare bird's nest or chasing after a butterfly. He doesn't care. He seems to be quite happy talking to himself.

I'll stop thinking about Beetle now or I'll start to worry in case he doesn't come today. Instead, I'll go back to remembering.

My father was far away from Magdala when the news came that the British had landed. He turned back for home at once, urging on his army and dragging his cannon with him. At the same time the British troops, with their elephants and mules and guns and tents and all their baggage, were scrambling up and down the mountainsides towards us from the north. A race was on to see who would get to Magdala first.

In all those weeks of waiting, nothing much changed for me. I remember a great buzz of talking and people coming and going. I was only interested in trying to avoid the whip my teacher liked to use on me when I forgot my Amharic letters.

There was one day, though, that I can see even now through a haze of golden light.

Father was still miles from home. I'd heard Samuel tell Mr Rassam that the British were sure to reach our mountain fortress first. I don't think Samuel liked living on Magdala very much. He probably wanted the British to free Mr Rassam so that they could both go away and he could be a servant in a grand British consulate.

The chiefs and princes who lived at my father's court were all gossiping about the rumours too. They were traitors at heart, all of them were, and they started plotting as they always did. Amma was afraid that they would slip off down into the valleys and join the rebellious tribes who were gathering there, waiting for a good moment to attack Father.

Amma set her women to make a feast. (I used to be able to smell the spices in my imagination, but I can't do it any more.) When it was ready she made me stand still while Abebech shaved the hair from my head, all except for a tuft on top and a fringe round my face. Then she dressed me in a new silk tunic, put a heavy silver necklace with a pendant cross round my neck and tucked a gold-handled dagger into the sash round my waist.

'Come, Alamayu,' she said, grasping my hand as we stepped out of the house together, with the guards bowing as we passed.

It was a great surprise to me, because Amma never usually went outside. When we had travelled with my father, he wouldn't allow anyone to see her or his other women. We had to go by night with a strong guard of eunuchs, who would make anyone we met on the road turn their backs until we had passed. If any man dared to come into our house without the King's permission, he would be killed at once.

I could feel that Amma was nervous. She was holding my hand so tightly that it felt painfully crushed, but I didn't dare say anything because her face was so set and determined.

We walked out of our compound towards the house where Father usually stayed. Amma had told the servants to spread out a sea of carpets in the open air and to build a dais at one end piled with cushions. A screen had been set up to one side. Amma slipped behind the screen before anyone could see her, pulling me after her, and we looked out through a crack in it.

The chiefs and their most important followers were waiting for us, sitting about on the carpets below the dais. Our servants were going round among them, passing out the food and drink.

Amma gave me a little shove.

'Go and sit on the dais,' she hissed in my ear. 'You're their prince. Show yourself to them. They've got to know that you're your father's heir. Don't wriggle about, Alamayu, but sit up straight, in the way I showed you. Don't move until I call for you.'

So I had to walk up to the dais in front of everyone and sit down on the cushions, while the umbrella of state was brought out from inside Father's house and opened above my head. Usually when I ran about Magdala those old men called out to me and petted me, picked me up and put their bristly faces against mine, but this time they were glancing sideways at each other and looking blankly at me. The silence was uneasy.

I kept looking over to the screen. Amma was hidden from the chiefs, but from the dais where I was sitting I could just see her. She was scanning the old men's faces and whispering to Gebre. They were checking to see who had come and who had stayed away. I think, too, that she was trying to work out who among them would be loyal to me.

An Abyssinian Chief

Those old chiefs knew what they had to do. It was a crafty one who stood up first. He spent several minutes arranging his *shamma* over his shoulders and clearing his throat. Then, leaning on his stick, he began a long speech, saying how he would serve the King until his dying breath and be loyal forever to his son, the Prince. I knew what I had to do too. I bowed my head, just a bit, like I had seen my father do.

The old man sat down and another one stood up, and another. I started yawning, but I knew that Amma's eyes were on me, so to keep myself awake I thought about what I would do when I was king. I decided that I'd punish any teachers who beat children just because they hadn't learned their letters, and that I'd make a law that boys could play with their catapults whenever they felt like it, and that there would always be honey for princes to eat.

The chiefs went on and on, and I ran out of ideas of kingly things to do. I remember thinking that if I'd have to spend all my time sitting still and listening to boring old men talking on and on, then I'd rather not grow up to be a king at all.

Gobezu, one of my father's lions, ambled up to the dais and flopped down beside me. Father was so strong and powerful that he could control his lions with no more than a look and a word of command, but I was never quite easy with them. I'd often seen them tearing to pieces goats and sheep which weren't much bigger than I was. But I wanted to look royal, so I put my hand on Gobezu's head. His fur was coarse and rough. I saw the chiefs' eyes widen when they looked at me, sitting up there with my hand on the head of a lion.

I had never felt so much like a prince before. I would never feel so much like a prince again.

When it was all over Amma sent for the chiefs who had stayed away. They arrived at our house one by one. They looked frightened. I think they had realized that she would tell Father that they had been disloyal. They bowed to the ground with sweat running down their faces. Amma didn't let them see her. She watched them through a hole in a curtain and called out to them to swear a loyal oath to the King and to me. And they all did just that, falling over themselves to get the words out quickly.

Everyone's afraid of Father, I thought.

I forgot how afraid of him I was myself. I felt nothing but pride.

Most of those chiefs didn't mean the promises they made that day. They didn't stand by their emperor when he needed them.

Father reached Magdala days before the British were sighted. In his bare feet he bounded up the steps cut into the rock and in through the lower gate, which the guards had flung wide open for him. He had left his followers far behind.

I had been waiting for him, hiding behind the inner gate. I was trembling, half excited, half scared, not knowing if he would pick me up in his arms and call me his darling, or cuff me painfully over the head and ask why I had run away from my teacher.

As soon as I saw his face I knew that it would be bad if he saw me, so I stayed hidden, shrinking further into the gap between the gate and the rock wall of the cliff. His eyes were red and staring, on fire with the rage that always frightened me.

I had hidden myself well and he raced on past me, towards the church. I crept after him and skulked about while the priests ran to bring carpets out to lay on the ground in front of the church. Then I saw my father seize a spear from one of the soldiers and drive it right through the carpet.

'That's what I'll do to those foreigners who have insulted me!' he screamed.

I didn't know if he meant his prisoners, like Mr Rassam, or the army of the British which was marching towards us, but somehow I thought he meant me, and in my fright I felt hot urine trickle down the inside of my leg. I ran home to Amma and buried my face in her lap.

Those last frantic days on Magdala are all scrambled up in a jumble to me now.

I see my father standing at the head of a cliff path while teams of men, leather ropes over their shoulders, haul up the steep slope, inch by inch, the huge gun which he

had forced the *ferenji* prisoners to make for him. I know I
haven't imagined it because I can still hear the men shout
and groan with effort, until Father raises his hand, just a
little way, and they fall silent at once.

I see the priests in their white robes and turbans, lined
up in rows, bowing and bobbing backwards and forwards
as they dance the dance of the psalms.

I see (and hear) the vultures wheeling and crying as they
dive down to feast on . . . But I won't think of those piles of
Abyssinian prisoners' bodies lying at the foot of the cliffs.

I see the European prisoners who, in his mercy, my
father had released from the heavy chains they had worn
for months around their ankles. They had forgotten how
to walk without the weight of them, and for the first day
or two they kept lifting their legs too high with each step.
They looked so funny, stumbling around, that I liked to
imitate them. I staggered about the house doing strange
hops and lurches, until Amma told me that such behaviour
was silly for a prince.

And then they came. The British Army came.

My father had gone down from the summit of Magdala,
where our house was, and was living in his scarlet silk tent
on the great flat plain of Selamge just below. A servant

came to our door one day and called in that the King of Kings wished to see the Queen, the Prince and the Lady Yetemegnu. We were all to go down to him.

There was a stupid flurry of course: clothes dragged out of chests, hair patted and combed – but before Amma was ready, another man came running to say that the Queen wasn't wanted after all, only the prince and Yetemegnu.

I can imagine now that Amma must have been angry about that. I didn't think of her, but only of myself. Half excited, half scared, I was too impatient to wait for fat Yetemegnu, so I made Gebre take me down to Selamge on my own.

It was always an adventure to go down to Selamge from the top of Magdala. Selamge was still high above the gorge through which ran the river below, and there were steep drops on three sides, but it was a very wide space, and flat, and there was plenty of room for my father's camp and his thousands of soldiers. I liked it especially because the horses were kept there and sometimes I was allowed to ride.

Father was sitting on a rock almost at the edge of the cliff, looking out across the abyss to the mountains on the far side. (No one in England could possibly imagine the mountains and canyons of my country, the cool clear air and the brilliant blue of the sky. There are no little green hills and cosy valleys in Abyssinia, no hedgerows and square-towered churches. There are no mists or fogs either.)

Some of the European prisoners were standing behind
Father, and for a moment I was afraid that they might even
push him over the edge of the cliff, but then I saw, from
the stiff way they were standing, that they were almost too
scared to move.

Emperor Theodore

They were like me, I suppose. They never knew what
the King's mood would be. Sometimes he would be on
fire with rage and have them chained up again. Sometimes

he was as kind and good as a best friend could ever be and would send his slaves to them with presents.

I hung back until I could see how it would be, but then I saw Father turn and smile at Mr Rassam, his favourite among the prisoners, and I knew it would be all right that day. I ran towards him and he laughed, picked me up and settled me on his knee.

There was nowhere in the world I liked better to be, than on my father's knee when he was in his gentle mood.

'Do you see, Alamayu?' he said, pointing to a distant gash running down the slope of the mountain on the far side of the gorge. 'Isn't that a fine road I built to bring my guns to Magdala? That's the way the British will come.'

I nodded, but I didn't care about the road.

'When they get here, you'll blow them all up, won't you, Father? Like this – whoosh!'

I made exploding movements with my hands.

Behind me I heard one of the foreigners groan and then turn the sound quickly into a cough. Father heard too. Nothing ever escaped his notice. Instead of being angry, he laughed.

'It'll be a great sight,' he said. 'A disciplined army. All the way here from Britain to our Abyssinia! You see how I forced them to come to me? What a spectacle it will be! We'll be astonished, all of us.' He paused and hunched his shoulders, letting his head sink down as he thought. 'What do you think, my son? If I let these men go –' he jerked his head to indicate the silent group behind him – 'will the British be grateful? If they are, perhaps they'll join me and help me defeat the rebels and all my enemies. What do you say, eh?'

He pushed his face right into mine. I smelled the heavy waft of *tej* on his breath, and knew that he'd been drinking. I was right, because he reached down for the half-empty flask beside his feet and took a long swig from it.

'Here, boy,' he said. 'Take a look yourself. Tell me if you see the British coming.'

He waved his arm and one of the slaves standing close by ran forward and put the King's telescope into my hands. It was so big and heavy that I could hardly lift it to my eye. Then I swung it around too fast, so that all I could see was blue sky, and after that a blur of brown rock and cliff.

'Rest it on my shoulder,' Father said. 'Hold it still.'

I got off his knee, climbed up on to the rock behind him and laid the telescope on his shoulder. Once it was steady, things leaped out towards me. I saw birds soaring across the face of a cliff and a man in the gorge far down below driving a few cows to drink in the river. Then I raised the telescope again, caught a movement, steadied it, and gasped.

'What? What have you seen?' The harshness in Father's voice startled me. He had leaped to his feet and now he wrenched the telescope out of my hands.

'Baboons, Father! There are lots and lots of them,

climbing on the rocks down there. I could see them so clearly, as if they were right here in front of us!'

His mood had suddenly changed. He pushed me roughly out of the way and swung the telescope round until it was pointing north, up a long, deep valley towards a distant cliff face. He took a step forward, and I was afraid he would go further and fall over the edge of the cliff, so I clutched at his *shamma* to haul him back. He shook me off.

'I can see them!' he cried hoarsely. 'They're coming! They're coming!'

He was trembling with excitement. The foreigners were trembling too, but with fear, and had stepped backwards.

Father's scornful look swept over them. 'Should I kill you?' he said quietly, as if he was talking to himself. 'If I do, perhaps the British will kill my son. So should I let you go?'

I blocked my mind to what he was saying, and anyway, I didn't care about the foreigners. I wanted to see if the rumour was true, that the British had brought elephants.

Father had set the telescope down on the ground. I picked it up and steadied it on the rock on which he had been sitting.

I couldn't see anything at first. I waved the telescope about, looking for big lumbering beasts. Then I saw something strange. Far, far away there was a flash of red. I held the telescope as still as I could.

Pinpricks of red. A glitter of sunlight on metal. A long moving line. The British were coming towards us, unstoppable and terrifying.

Father snatched the telescope from me and handed it to one of the prisoners.

'Here come the donkeys!' he shouted. 'You see them? Coming here to kill me?'

I didn't wait for more. Father was walking restlessly about, and his face – but I can't bear to think of that now. Nightmares lurk in my father's face.

I moved cautiously backwards, hoping not to be noticed, then turned and ran as fast as I could, past the line of heavy cannon and the rows of soldiers' tents, past the tethered horses and the huts of the thousands of cooks and servants.

'Wait, Prince! Don't go so fast!' a squeaky voice called out, and I looked back and saw Gebre panting along after me. I ran back to him, relieved. Gebre was only a slave, but I had known him all my life. He had always been kind to me. He loved me; I know he did.

'They're all red,' I said to him.

'Who?'

'The British. I saw them. They're red.'

He took my hand. I wondered why his palm was so clammy. I think it must have been nervous sweat.

'The King your father will send them back to their own country crying like women.'

'I know.'

But I didn't know. I knew nothing at all. And from that moment, nothing in my life was ever certain again.

The British Army on the march in Abyssinia

My father didn't call me down to Selamge again during the next few days. I wasn't sure if I was glad or sorry. I would have been scared to be with him if the anger was still on him, but I wanted him to reassure me too. In any case, nothing was comfortable at home. Amma was ill all the time. She lay with her eyes shut, her whole body shaken by fits of coughing, while Abebech coaxed her to eat. If she did find the strength to sit up, she would call for her books and sit reading, then shut her eyes and rock backwards and forwards as she prayed. Yetemegnu had never taken much notice of me, and she didn't now. Abebech was irritable with me too. All her attention was taken up by Amma.

Even my tutor, who was usually so harsh and ready with his whip, seemed distracted. After a day or two he stopped coming to our house at all. No one seemed to notice whether I was at home or not, so I took to slipping out whenever Abebech's back was turned. If I could get past Gebre and the eunuch guards, I was free to wander where I liked around the mountain top.

I peeped into the houses where the European prisoners lived, wondering about the strange plants they had grown in their compounds, but I never went near the crowded prison huts of the Abyssinian prisoners. The stench and sounds of misery frightened me too much.

I was drawn all the time to the cliff edge from where I could look down on Selamge. I could sometimes make out Father in the distance. I saw him one day directing men to rearrange his cannon, bringing them forward and changing the angle of the barrels.

I often looked in the direction where I had seen the red uniforms and the metal weapons, but without a telescope I couldn't make out anything, and sometimes I thought I must have only imagined those blurs of colour and glancing points of light. Then one evening, when the sun had gone around to the south, I was lying on my stomach, watching the crowds on Selamge below milling round my father's scarlet tent. There was an unfamiliar sound behind me. I looked round and saw a horrible sight. Oh, why can't I forget it?

The Abyssinian prisoners were being herded towards the steep path that led down from Magdala to Selamge, and I realized that Father must have ordered them to be taken down to him. They were as thin as skeletons, shuffling along in their heavy chains, some too weak to walk without leaning on each other. There were old men and young men and women too.

I put my hands over my ears to block out their groans and looked down towards Selamge again. The evening sun was shining directly on to the steep mountainside on the far side of the canyon below. And the mountainside was moving.

I shaded my eyes. I could see big, lurching masses of grey. Elephants! So it was true. The British knew how to tame elephants! There were mules too, and huge guns, and men! So many men!

I felt sick. I wanted to get up and run home, but the line of prisoners, hundreds of them, was in the way, and I hated the thought of getting close to them.

I did what I have done many, many times since that day. I went inside myself. I looked down at the tiny patch of ground just in front of my eyes and watched an ant pick up a heavy seed and carry it away. I stared at that ant, concentrating all my thoughts on it, as if its tiny body and the seed that it carried, were the only things that mattered in the world.

'Your father was a murderer,' a Rugby boy said to me once. 'I heard what he did. Three hundred prisoners, in cold blood. He threw them over a cliff, didn't he, one by one?'

I don't listen when people say things like that. The ant trying to carry his seed swims up before my eyes. I walk away. What else can I do? I don't know why Father killed his prisoners. I know he had been drinking again. I know he was sorry afterwards.

'His valet said he didn't sleep at all that night,' I heard

Yetemegnu tell my mother. 'He was drunk. He kept saying, "Am I a tyrant to my people? Will God punish me?" He prayed in agony without closing his eyes until dawn broke.'

Who could understand Father, when he didn't understand himself? He was loved and hated. He was feared and adored. He was a king, but he liked simple things, plain food and ordinary clothes, and he hated fuss and luxury.

Amma didn't approve of that.

'A king should look like a king,' she grumbled to Abebech, but she said it quietly, so that no spy would overhear and report her disloyal words. She would lower her voice even further and say, 'It's hardly surprising that he behaves like a peasant. You've only got to look at his mother.'

I think that Amma, who almost never went outside and sat at home most of the time, was wrong about Father. He didn't need silk robes and a crown in order to look like a king. He could run faster than any man in Abyssinia, and he was stronger than his strongest soldier. I'd often seen him leap with one bound from the ground into the saddle of Hamra, his big bay horse, without touching the stirrups at all.

(I tried doing that once, in the stables at Freshwater,

before I came to Rugby. No one was looking. I took a run at Blackie, my pony, and jumped as high as I could, but I crashed into Blackie's flank and fell to the ground. By the time I'd picked myself up, Blackie had reared in fright and was bolting round the stable yard. I had to chase after him and give him sugar lumps to calm him down. I never told anyone, not even Captain Speedy. I was afraid he would laugh.)

Soon after I'd seen the prisoners shuffle past I was called down to Selamge again, and I went, holding tight to Gebre's hand, not knowing what would happen. I think Father had been studying the British soldiers through his telescope, and he'd been impressed by their red coats and smart white helmets. Whatever the reason, he had dressed like a king, and was wearing a silk tunic with gold thread running through it and white trousers made of a shining material.

It wasn't the magnificence of Father's clothes that I remember that day though. It was the strength and will in his face and his voice. All his thousands of soldiers were lined up to listen to him. They were our best men. Sometimes in the past I'd watched them march out with him to war. He always rode at their head on his warhorse. The cavalry used to come behind him, with the foot soldiers and the baggage train and all the thousands of followers bringing up the rear. A forest of spears jogged up and down in the hands of the warriors as they rode or ran in the king's wake, and sunlight danced on the metal bosses of their shields, like sparks of fire.

I thought that Father was about to lead his army out against the invaders straight away. I imagined that his men would race down the mountainside, yelling their blood-curdling war cries, and kill all the British then and there. Instead he leaped up on to a rock. I shall never forget how he stood there against the sky, with one of the great cliffs falling away behind him. His head was thrown back and the breeze ruffled his shimmering silk clothes. When he spoke, his voice rang out into the clear air.

'Very soon we will be fighting an army of great strength with weapons much better than our own,' he cried. 'Even the clothes of our enemies are decorated with gold! I have seen them through my telescope. They have brought with them so much treasure that only elephants are strong enough to carry it.'

A sigh – almost a groan – had gone round at the mention of the British guns, but the men liked the idea of treasure.

'Are you ready to fight?' Father called out. His voice had deepened, and even now I shiver and feel the hairs rise on my arms as I remember it. 'Will you do battle, and become rich with the treasure of these white slaves, or will you abandon me and disgrace us all?'

An old chief jumped up and made a silly speech, I don't remember what. I was standing stock still, gripped by excitement. Every nerve in my body was on fire. If someone at that moment had put a gun or a sword in my hands, I would have run down on my short legs to the British camp far below and attacked the first soldier I could see.

I waited for Father to send his troops racing down the mountainside to attack the British straight away, but he didn't. After a while the troops milling around him quietly moved away.

The exhilaration left me and all I could feel was fear. Until that moment, in spite of all the talk of the approaching army, and the strange tales of how they could send messages to each other from miles away with special machines, and how they had tamed elephants, and how they had built a wagon that could run on metal lines across the land and carry men and goods, I hadn't understood that a battle would have to be fought. For days there had been a crackling tension in the air at home and the servants had been packing my mother's precious books and jewellery along with all our clothes, but I'd never quite imagined that the British guns would be firing at *us*, at *me*, and that Father's strength and courage were the only things that stood between me and a terrible unknown future.

I think I sat down suddenly on the ground, and I know I nearly burst into tears, though I was trying hard not to, because crying made Father angry. At any rate, I wasn't there for long, because Gebre grabbed my arm in an almost painful grip and hauled me to my feet, and I trotted wordlessly beside him, back up the steep path from Selamge to our home on Magdala above.

The next day seemed strangely normal, except that everyone was annoyed with me. I spent it, like most other days, at home. We lived and slept in the long room that ran right along the upper story of our house. Pillars stretched down the length of it, and our beds were tucked between them. There was a covered veranda along one side, and I used to like bouncing up and down on the boards there to make them squeak. Amma spent the day sitting at one end of the room on her beautiful cushions, and Yetemegnu usually stayed at the other end. When my teacher came, he and I sat downstairs under the veranda, because Amma said the sound of me chanting the letters irritated her.

My tutor hadn't come that day, and I had nothing to do. I wanted to run outside, then climb up to the watchtower in the corner of our compound to see what was happening, but no one would let me do anything. They were at me all day long.

'No, Alamayu, you can't go out of the house. It's too dangerous. The British might attack at any moment.'

'Stop banging those sticks together, Alamayu. You're making my head ache.'

'Out of my way, dear. How can I pack all these clothes with you sprawled across them like that?'

Anger must have been building up in me, because in

the end I started crying and I couldn't stop. I screamed, I think, and beat out with my fists at anyone who came near me. I know I was slapped by Amma, who burst into tears herself, and then I was picked up and cuddled by Abebech, and finally taken down the stairs by Gebre to the kitchen huts behind our house, where one of the cooks put a spoonful of honey into my mouth.

At last I fell asleep, tired out, still hiccuping from the sobs that had shaken me. And the next day was Friday, Good Friday, in fact, two days before Easter, but it would be a bad Friday for me, and for Abyssinia.

The sun had risen high in the sky when at last I opened my eyes on that fateful day. No one seemed to notice that I was awake. No one made me wash my face or brought me any food. I was indignant in my childish way, feeling ignored, and I thought about crying again, but I understood that everyone in the house – Amma, Yetemegnu, Abebech, Gebre, the other eunuchs, slaves and hangers-on – were all on such an edge of fear and dread that I would get nothing but slaps and curses.

I looked round to make sure that no one could see me, opened the heavy door on to the veranda, crept along the boards on tiptoe, trying not to make them creak, then

ran down the stairway. No one noticed me or called me
to come back. I dashed round to the kitchen huts behind
the house, where usually the cooks made a big fuss of me.
It was a fasting day, being Good Friday, so there was no
honey, but one of them silently put into my hands some
of last night's supper, and I squatted down to eat it, only
to find that I wasn't hungry after all. A strange knot in my
stomach seemed to be taking up all the room.

I wanted to go the edge of the cliff and look down on
to Selamge to see what was happening. I guessed that the
guards on the compound entrance would be too jumpy
today to let me out, as they often did on ordinary days,
so I sidled round to where there was a hole in the thorn
fence just big enough for me to squeeze through. It was
uncomfortable and scratchy, but I got out all right.

There was a strange quietness up there on the flat
mountain top of Magdala. I found out afterwards that
many people had slipped away during the night and made
their way down the far side of the mountain from Selamge.
In my opinion they were cowards, to desert their King.
They'd flattered and crawled to Father for years, but they
showed their true nature in the end.

The huts of the Abyssinian prisoners were empty of
course. They had all been sent to their deaths. The eerie
silence round their compound scared me. No sounds
came from the European prisoners' huts. The *ferenjis* were
keeping themselves well out of sight. I suppose they were

frightened that they would be the next ones to die.

I went to the edge of the cliff and lay down in my favourite place. There was so much going on down below that I didn't know which way to look. Our soldiers were busy everywhere. Some were dragging the cannon down to a flat bit of land that jutted out over the gorge. Others were carrying ammunition. The foot soldiers were cleaning their muskets and sharpening the tips of their spears. The cavalry horses were being saddled. Priests were moving about among the people, and the men stopped what they were doing to bow over the priests' hand-crosses and kiss them.

What surprised me was the clothes the cavalry officers were wearing. They had put on red shirts! Red silk shirts! I felt proud when I saw that. I thought that our men could match the British in anything, even in the colour of their clothes, and I was sure that we would beat them easily, in spite of their elephants and their machines.

Overhead, clouds in fantastic shapes were piled like huge black and white castles, blocking out the sun. The light had dazzled my eyes before, but without the brilliance everything was actually clearer. I could see beyond Selamge to the gorge below.

I gasped at the sight. Long lines of men were moving towards our position. The enemy was creeping up the steep flanks of the mountainside. Some had guns in their hands. Some were leading mules, whose heads nodded as they struggled to climb the rugged path under their heavy loads of long, strange pipes.

Father won't know they're coming! He won't have seen them! I thought.

I scrambled to my feet, ready to run down and warn him, but then I felt a hand catch my tunic at the neck.

'Prince!' It was Gebre. 'What are you doing out here? You must come back with me at once.'

I could see that he was angry. Being a slave, he didn't dare to shout at me, but he looked quite ferocious with fury. I tried to wriggle out of his grasp, but he wrapped his arms tightly round my chest and lifted me up so that my feet kicked out helplessly into the air.

'Let me go!' I yelled. 'Let me *go*! The *ferenji* soldiers are creeping up Selamge! Look down there! I've got to tell Father!'

Gebre's grip didn't slacken, but he peered over my tossing head and I heard him take a deep breath. He was quiet for a long moment. Then he let out his breath and said, 'Look. Our scouts have seen them. They're running to tell His Majesty.'

He relaxed his arms a little and I nearly escaped. He was too quick for me though. He squeezed me so tight that I could hardly breathe.

'We must get away from here,' he said, panic in his voice.

'No! Look! There's Father! He's riding Hamra!'

The cavalry had mounted now and were lined up to one side. The thousands of foot soldiers were pushing at each other as they tried to get near the King. They carried muskets and spears in their hands, and their *shammas* were thrown back over their shoulders. Father was riding Hamra on a tight rein, making the lovely bay horse high-step down the lines of his men and back again. The wind, which was blowing the clouds in from the east, threw snatches of his words towards us, and I could tell that Gebre was held in the spell of Father's majesty as much as I was. He stopped trying to pull me away.

'My children,' Father shouted, 'don't be afraid of these English soldiers!' He turned and his words were lost in the wind. Then he wheeled Hamra round again. '. . . in the name of God, I shall conquer!'

I could see the mules of the British clearly now, appearing from the steep path below, and the *ferenjis* with them were racing to unload heavy boxes from the animals' backs.

'Has God not appointed me to be the King of Kings?' Father was shouting. 'I am the old hero in battle! I am . . .' He turned again. When I next heard him he was declaring, 'In the name of the Father, and of the Son, and of the Holy Ghost, I tell you that all who die in battle today shall have their sins forgiven!'

'*Jan Hoy*,' Gebre was murmuring reverently. '*Jan Hoy*! His Majesty!'

Father turned now. He was facing his soldiers but pointing over his shoulder to the British troops, who were pouring up the slope behind him. For a moment I was confused. Most of them weren't wearing red uniforms after all, but the dull greeny brown colour they call khaki.

'Look at those slaves!' Father was yelling. 'They're nothing but women! They're bringing you clothes and treasure and money! Go down, my children, and help yourselves!'

The men were cheering wildly now. They broke away from Father and began to race down the slope towards the enemy. They were a moving wave of white, with the scarlet of the officers' silks glowing like poppies among them.

A cloud of smoke billowed out from the mouth of one of Father's cannon as it rocked back on its undercarriage, and a second later a fearsome boom was echoing backwards and forwards between the cliffs.

I felt Gebre's arms tremble. He began to run with me back towards our house. I didn't struggle any longer. My heart was pounding with such fright that I thought it would jump out of my chest. I flung my arms round Gebre's neck and clung to him as tightly as I could.

There's a question I don't usually dare to ask myself. Where was God on that day when the British rifles cut down our soldiers? He seemed to be speaking during those terrible hours – thunder was rolling through the clouds, and rain and hail poured down from the sky – but we were never sure if it was God's voice we were hearing, or the rage of the guns.

I spent the hours while the battle raged in our house, sitting as close as I could to Amma, clinging to her with all my strength, my arms round her neck, and hers tight around me. We rocked backwards and forwards together. Sometimes, if a bang was particularly loud, and she didn't know if it was thunder right overhead or a shell landing near our house, she would cry out, 'Aiee! God protect us! For the sake of Mary!'

At first one of the eunuchs ran in every few minutes with news:

'Our men are far more numerous than the enemy!'

'His Majesty is firing his cannon!'

After a while no one came.

A long time later, a few notes of strange music made me prick up my ears. It was the first time I'd heard a bugle call. The British Army uses them like a language. Now I know that this one meant, 'Cease fire!'

There was an eerie silence after that.

Since then I've heard that the British rifles were almost red hot from firing round after round into the unprotected bodies of our soldiers, and that after the ceasefire the British fixed bayonets on to their rifle barrels and swept forward to the final kill. The ground was covered with our dead and wounded. Our ancient muskets and spears had been useless against the British rifles. Father's greatest cannon, which the men had hauled with such effort up the cliff faces, had exploded when it fired its first round. Our officers, in their red shirts, had made easy targets for the British. Most of them were dead.

Stupid Yetemegnu started shouting, 'They'll come for us now! The British will catch us now! White devils! Oh God, God, help us!'

God wasn't listening to any of our prayers, but at least He did then make the thunder roll away. He even gave us a little sad sunshine at the end of that dreadful day. Darkness falls quickly in Abyssinia. It was soon night time, and we still knew nothing for certain.

The day after the battle it was as if the storm of the afternoon before had never happened. The British had beaten our troops and killed our best men, but they were still below Selamge, on another stretch of flat ground lower down the mountain. They hadn't yet dared to storm the steep paths and gates that would bring them up to Magdala.

As the sun rose over the horizon I ran out on to the veranda and looked out. The sky was bright and clear. A bird, sitting on the thorn fence, was shrilling loudly. I caught a whiff of woodsmoke and ran down the stairs to the kitchen huts. Smoke was curling up through the thatch of one of them. I looked in through the door. Only one old woman was there, poking sticks into the fire and bending down to blow them into a flame.

'Where are the other cooks?' I asked.

She straightened up, peered at me and said, 'They've run away! All run away!' Then she burst out into a cackle of laughter so loud that I was frightened and ran back to our house.

Gebre was sitting on the bottom step of the staircase that led up to our veranda. He was holding his head in his hands and groaning.

For some reason, all I could think about was Hamra, my father's horse.

'Is Hamra all right?' I asked him. 'Is Father going to ride him again today?'

Gebre didn't seem to hear me. In any case, he didn't look up. I was annoyed. Servants were supposed to stand up whenever they were in my presence. Then I became aware of another sound from far away, quite unlike the sound of the bird still singing away on the thorn fence. People were wailing. I was getting angrier.

'Gebre!' I shouted.

He looked up at last and scrambled to his feet. I saw that his hair was standing in uncombed spikes round his head and that tears had made lines through the smears of dirt on his cheeks. He looked down at me, but didn't seem to see me.

'Is Hamra all right?' I demanded again.

'Hamra?' he repeated stupidly. 'How should I know?'

I landed a feeble kick on his shin.

'You're silly,' I said, and ran inside to find Amma.

I didn't know then that Gebre's brother was lying dead on the slopes below, and that hyenas had worried at his body during the night.

'Amma, the cooks have all gone, except one old one, and Gebre's not talking properly, and where are the guards? There's only one at the gate.'

Yetemegnu had been squatting beside Amma. They had had their heads together, talking. It had almost looked as if they were friends. Now she lumbered to her feet.

'Only one guard? So we're unprotected now! When the *ferenji* soldiers come . . .'

Her voice tailed away.

It was already quite late in the day when a messenger ran up to the last eunuch standing at our gate, said something to him, turned and ran away again. The eunuch rushed into the house, and I followed him.

'A message from His Majesty, Your Highness,' he said to Amma. 'The King wants to see you, and the Prince. You have to go down to Selamge right away.'

Yetemegnu pushed herself forward.

'And me? Surely he wants me?'

'Not you. Only the Queen and the Prince.'

I had been enjoying a game, I remember, and I didn't want to stop playing it. I nearly opened my mouth to protest, but one look at Amma's face silenced me. She picked up her *shamma*, draped it round her head, held out her hand for mine and was ready.

'Aren't you going to change your dress?' I said. 'And this is my old tunic, look.'

She didn't bother to answer. She was already dragging me out of the house. Then she dropped my hand and ran for the gatehouse which stood at the top of the steep path running down from Magdala to Selamge. It was as much as I could do to keep up with her.

There were still a dozen or more guards at the upper gatehouse. They all knew me by sight.

'You can't go down there, Prince,' one of them said to me. 'We have orders to let no one through.'

'You must,' I told him. 'The King has sent for me and my mother.'

He looked over to Amma. She was standing still, her

face shrouded in her *shamma*, and his jaw dropped as he realized who she was. He ran to the gate to open it, then called to two of the men to escort us.

I had been feeling happy until then, thinking that as soon as we saw Father all the strange things that had been happening, all the frightened voices and loud noises, wouldn't be there any more. I thought that everything would go back to normal, but as we hurried on down the steep rocky path, I began to feel scared again. There wasn't room for me to walk beside Amma, so I couldn't go on holding her hand. She had pushed me on to run in front of her.

I hung back. She said something to one of the guards and he picked me up and carried me the rest of the way.

I suppose the thing that had scared me was the sound of weeping and the funeral songs rising up from all around Selamge. From the height of the guard's shoulder I could look down over the whole of Father's camp. Everything seemed to be in a mess. Tents were half toppled over, and further down the slope men were lying on the ground. People were pulling at lifeless bodies, crying over them and trying to carry them away. Others were squatting in little groups, holding on tightly to their spears.

The flaps of Father's red tent were closed. The guard put me down. Wolde, Father's body servant, was standing outside, shaking out one of Father's white *shammas*. Amma nudged me, and I asked him where Father was. He jerked his chin towards a boulder a little way away.

Father was sitting on it. He seemed to be talking to himself. A row of important-looking men stood near him. They were watching him over their shoulders and murmuring to each other. One of them saw us, went over to Father, bent down and whispered in his ear. Father jumped to his feet and hurried across to us.

I waited till I could see what mood he was in before I dared run to him, but I couldn't read the expression in his eyes so I stayed close by Amma's side.

'Get inside the tent,' he said curtly to Amma. 'How could you come so openly without a proper escort? Everyone can see you!'

She laughed bitterly. 'What does that matter now?'

But she went into the tent. He followed her, and I crept inside after them.

It felt peculiar to be with both my parents at once. It had only happened to me a few times before. As they stood staring at each other, the sun shone through the red walls of the tent and made their faces and clothes glow with a strange warmth.

Father said nothing for a moment. Then he sighed.

'Tirunesh. Tirunesh!'

Not many people ever used her name. I wasn't used to hearing it.

'How are you?' Father went on. 'Are you well? How have you been?'

It was what he said to everyone. It was just the way

we greet each other, even strangers, in my language. He seemed to be searching for the real words he wanted to say.

He came out with them at last.

'I haven't been . . . good to you. I haven't been a faithful husband.'

Amma was staring at the carpet which covered the floor of the tent. She said nothing.

'But why weren't you kinder to me?' Father burst out. 'You never loved me as a wife should! You were scornful of me and my family!'

I was staring up at them. They were giants to me. Amma's eyes were still lowered, but I saw tears slide down her cheeks. I was afraid that Father would see them and be angry. He was always angry with me if I cried, but he wasn't angry now. He took her hand and led her gently to a stool. She sat down on it and he sat on the carpet, cross-legged, looking up at her.

'It's over,' he said. 'You know that.'

She nodded. 'What are you going to do?' she whispered.

He ignored the question.

'The British were too strong for me. They were sent by a queen, a woman, and I thought her soldiers would be like women too. My men were like lions! They never hesitated. But we had no weapons! And the British rifles – I've never seen anything to equal them. The *ferenjis* can shoot and reload in a couple of seconds. I've lost all my best people. My old friends. Men who had been with me on all my campaigns.'

Amma was looking down into his eyes, and her face was soft, almost as if she was looking at me.

'Theodore, I'm sorry too,' she said. 'I should have been a better wife to you.'

He smiled, put up a finger and smudged away the tears drying on her cheeks.

'Well, well. It's too late for all that now. We have to decide what to do with you and the boy.'

'We'll stay with you!' Amma declared, her voice loud again.

'No. That won't be possible.' He paused, thinking. 'I suppose you could go back to your father's country. To Semyen.'

He stood up and began to pace round the tent, biting his thumb as he thought.

'That won't do. It's too dangerous. You'd never get that far. My enemies are all around us. And I don't only mean the British. Think of the rebels! South, west . . . they're everywhere. The boy's my heir. Any one of them would kill him if they got their hands on him.'

Amma gasped and pulled her *shamma* over her mouth. I felt fear prickle all over my skin and pressed myself against her.

Father stopped pacing and frowned down at her.

'You see that, don't you, Tirunesh?'

He went to the door of the tent and called out, 'Wolde!'

'*Abet? Jan Hoy!*' Wolde called back.

'The letter from the British general. Where is it?'

Wolde came into the tent. Politely keeping his eyes away from Amma, he sidled round behind her and pulled a letter out of the satchel hanging from a hook on the tent post. He put it into Father's hands and slipped outside again.

I stood on tiptoe to look. I could see that the top half of the paper had strange letters written on it, but there were proper Amharic letters at the bottom.

Father was scanning the page and talking to himself.

'Where is that bit? "Your Majesty has fought like a brave man . . ." Hmph! Fine words! "If Your Majesty will submit to the Queen of England . . ." Here we are. Listen to this, Tirunesh. "I guarantee honourable treatment for yourself and for all the members of Your Majesty's family." He guarantees honourable treatment, you see? For you and Alamayu.'

Amma was staring at him, open-mouthed.

'You want me to surrender myself, and my son, to *them*? To the *British*?'

'It's the safest thing.'

'I won't do it. I can't.'

No one ever refused an order from Father. His eyebrows twitched together in a frown. Then he took a deep breath and said, 'What else do you propose to do, Tirunesh? What other solution is there?'

'I told you. We'll stay with you.'

'And I told you that won't be possible.'

'You want him to be brought up by *ferenjis*? Theodore, you cannot be serious.'

'You want him to be murdered by one of my – *many* – enemies?' he shot back.

My head was going backwards and forwards from one to the other. They were talking about me. I was desperate to know what it all meant.

Amma got to her feet. She was biting her lip. I was still clinging to her, and now she crushed me into her side. She said nothing for a long time, her eyes fixed on Father's face. At last she let out a long breath.

'You're right,' she said, sinking back down on to her stool. 'It's the only way.'

He smacked his right fist into his left hand, triumphant and relieved.

'Not immediately,' he said. 'There's still hope. I've written to Napier – the general's name is Napier, apparently. I'll send him a handsome gift. Cows and sheep. His men must be desperate for meat by now. If he accepts them, it might still end well. He might even, you never know, give me some proper weapons. Help me defeat the rebels.'

She shook her head at him disbelievingly.

He didn't notice. He drew up another stool, sat down on it and beckoned me over to him. I stood between his knees and rested my two palms on his muscular thighs. I could feel the hard sinews beneath the cloth.

'Alamayu!' he said.

I find it hard to believe even now, but I think his voice almost broke. He snatched me off my feet and hugged me tightly. I could feel his chest rise and fall as he took in some deep, hasty breaths. Then he set me down again, put a finger under my chin to lift my face and looked down earnestly into my eyes.

'You're a big boy now. Growing up fast.'

'Yes, Father.'

'You must listen to me carefully, Alamayu. The British have won the first battle against me. They'll try to storm Magdala itself now. Don't be afraid. They won't hurt you. If they succeed, and if . . . I'm no longer there, you'll be going on a long journey, with Amma. Over the sea, to the *ferenji* queen. The British will look after you. They'll teach you many things over there, my son. Learn what you can. Work hard.'

And then he said the words that have rung in my ears ever since. Words I will never forget.

'Always remember that you are a prince of Abyssinia, son of Theodore, the King of Kings.'

I knew my chin was wobbling. I tried to control it.

'Grow up to be strong. Be loyal to your friends. Be hard on your enemies. One day, who knows . . .'

His eyes had strayed beyond me, out through the

billowing flaps of the tent, to the mountain ranges rippling away into the distance.

'You are my heir,' he said, so softly I could barely hear him. 'You have the right to my throne.'

At least, I think that's what he said. To be truthful, I can't be sure how much of all that passed in the tent that day really happened, or how much I've made up, in my dreams and in my imagination. I'm sure, though, about what happened next.

Father stood up. He spoke quickly now, sounding curt, as if he was addressing his soldiers.

'Take him back up to Magdala, Tirunesh. Forgive me for all the wrong I've done you. Whatever you decide to do with the boy, you know my wishes. There is one thing above all. Make sure that he grows up to be a Christian. Keep heathen beliefs away from him. I know that in this at least he is in safe hands.'

Amma had started crying again. She seemed to have understood something I had not.

'God bless you,' she said. 'I forgive you, and you should forgive me. Alamayu will never forget you; I'll make sure of that.'

Father had turned away from us.

'Go on, quickly. Leave now.' His voice sounded thick.

I suddenly remembered the question I had wanted to ask him.

'Is Hamra all right, Father? Did the cannon scare him?

Will you teach me to ride him one day?'

But Amma had already wrapped her *shamma* closely round her head and was dragging me out of the tent, ready to hurry me back up the path to Magdala and home. I looked back, hoping that Father would answer my question, but he had dropped back down on to his stool, and his head was deep in his hands.

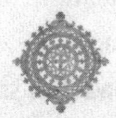

Whose face is this? Who is leaning over my bed, frightening me? A mouth is opening and shutting, saying words that I can't hear. Is it Father? Or Mother? Have they come to fetch me home?

A hand reaches out and something cool is laid on my burning forehead. Yes, I can see the face clearly now. It belongs to Nurse Thomson.

'Alamayu, dear,' she's saying, 'you're burning up. Drink a little water.'

But I can't. I turn my head away.

Don't bother me now, I want to say. Let me go back home.

I heard later that Father couldn't bear to stay inside his tent
that night. He rammed the blades of two spears into the
ground, strung a *shamma* between them and slept for an
hour or two on the bare ground beneath. He had the great
hardiness of a soldier. He never felt the cold or noticed the
dampness of the dew.

I saw too, with my own eyes, that when the moon rose
it was the colour of blood. It was an evil omen. Everyone
knew that.

I suppose I slept as usual on that last night in my old
home, under my blanket, on my mat. I only remember
that when morning came I ran out to the watchtower in
the corner of our compound. I wasn't usually allowed to
approach it, never mind climb it, but for once there was no
one around to stop me, and, a little nervously in case I was
seen and punished, I stole up the steep steps.

I had to stand on tiptoe to see out across the low wall
that surrounded the platform at the top. I thought of
scrambling up to sit on it, with my legs dangling down the
outside, but I was afraid that someone would see me and
shout at me to come down.

There was plenty to look at from this vantage point.
Outside our compound people were loading bundles on
to the backs of pack animals. I amused myself for a while
watching a frisky mule, which was kicking out at the man
trying to tie a sack to its back. The sack kept on slipping
and the man kept on shouting, until at last the sack fell to

the ground and burst open, and the flour inside it started to blow around, turning the man and the mule a funny pale colour.

When I looked beyond them I could see long strings of people, horses, mules and donkeys streaming out from Magdala, winding down the steep rocky paths. Those deserters were bold enough to walk straight past the rows of British tents pitched on the shelf of ground below Selamge.

I was shocked to see how many *ferenji* tents there were now, hundreds of little white cones in neat rows. And I shivered at the sight of the many red coats moving about among them.

Would they come today? Would they rush up and seize our house and take us away today?

I was distracted by the sight of the elephants. They were carrying huge loads of metal on their backs, great wheels and long brass tubes. They were not far away now, moving up on to the lower end of Selamge itself, closer and closer to where Father was, with the remnants of his army. I could see clearly how the men leading them made them kneel down so that the pipes could be offloaded. I wanted to run down, I remember, and touch the elephants, to feel their wrinkled grey sides beneath my fingers. I wanted know if their tusks were sharp.

I was so busy thinking about the elephants that I didn't take much notice of what the men were doing with the wheels and the tubes they had brought. How could I know

that they were assembling them into heavy guns? I didn't
understand that they were preparing to use them against
the cliffs of Magdala, ready to seize our mountain top in
one final assault.

I wasn't the only one who didn't understand because I
could see a large crowd standing on the cliff edge, looking
down curiously on what was happening on Selamge
below. I was tired of being alone, so I jumped down the
watchtower steps and ran across towards the crowd. There
was a mass of broad backs in front of me, and I was just
choosing a spot through which I could force my way, when
someone called out, 'It's the Prince! Prince Alamayu! Let
him come through!'

Then a man bent down and pushed his face so close to
mine that I could smell his rotting breath.

'Come to see what your father's brought upon us all,
have you?' he said. 'Come to gloat over us poor people?'

'Leave the boy alone,' a woman said, grabbing my arm.
'He's only a child. He's not to blame.'

'Look!' someone shouted. 'His Majesty!'

The woman relaxed her grip on my arm and I was
relieved to see that everyone had lost interest in me. I
wormed my way through to the front of the crowd.

The British were creeping up Selamge, sinister,
unstoppable, like the waters of a scarlet and khaki flood
rising and rising on the incoming tide. They were still half
a mile away from Father's camp, I suppose. I could see him

now. He was standing on his own, watching them approach through his telescope. Then I saw his groom run up to him, leading Hamra by the bridle. Father turned, and with his usual incredible energy leaped straight from the ground into the saddle.

It was the middle of the day, I think. At any rate, the sun was overhead and very hot. The light glittered on Father's shirt of golden silk, and on his lion-skin cape and his belt stuck with a pistol and a sword. He had dressed once more like a king.

Holding Hamra on a tight rein, he spurred the horse into a furious gallop across the highest part of Selamge, then wheeled him round and rode back again.

'What's he up to now?' the people around me were asking. 'Is he shouting? What's that he's saying?'

Hamra turned, and for a moment Father was facing the cliff along which we stood. The wind picked up his words and carried them clearly up to us.

'Send out a champion!' he was shouting. 'One man! One man!'

The man next to me let out a cackle of admiring laughter and smacked his hands down on to his thighs.

'Look at that! It's insane! He's asking for single combat!'

'*Jan Hoy!*' the people around me began to murmur. 'What courage, to defy the *ferenjis*! Doesn't he understand that they've already won? What a king! What a man!'

I didn't see the puffs of white smoke blossoming from

the mouths of those hastily assembled big British guns. I didn't know they had fired until a deafening explosion nearly knocked me off my feet. Another crash came, and then another. People all around me were screaming and running for cover. I stood still, too petrified to move.

I might have stayed there forever if someone, I don't know who it was, hadn't snatched me up and carried me away. They put me down at the entrance to the King's House and I stood there rigid, not even crying, until Gebre came out and found me. He dragged me across the courtyard, up the staircase to the veranda, and thrust me through the door into the great room.

Amma came running.

'Thank God! You're safe! Where have you been?'

I know now that the fearsome booms and crashes splitting the air all around us were the explosions of the shells spat out by the great British guns to shatter our mountain top, but at the time it seemed to me as if the whole world was breaking apart, and I thought that everything was coming to an end, that Satan had been loosed from hell and was hurling thunderbolts at us. I thought he was going to roll up the whole earth into the fires of destruction.

Yetemegnu was screaming uncontrollably, holding on to a pillar with one hand and beating her breast with the other. Amma went up to her and slapped her hard on the face.

'Stop that! We can't stay here. Did you hear me? Did

you hear that bomb? One's landed right below us in our courtyard. They're aiming at this house. We've got to get away. The foreign prisoners' compound is the safest place. Mr Rassam's house. They'll leave that part alone.'

The shock of the slap had stopped Yetemegnu's screams. She stared at Amma open-mouthed for a minute, put up a hand to rub her stinging cheek and seemed to shake herself into action. 'You're right.'

Then she turned and shrieked, 'Abebech! Where is that woman? Abebech! Get some people to carry out our things. Be quick!'

She bent down towards me, but I shrank from her as I always did.

'Tirunesh, leave all the bundles to me. Take the boy. I'll follow you. Just get him somewhere safe.'

Another explosion from just below the house almost deafened us, and I felt the walls creak and the boards of the floor shiver under my feet. Amma was out of the door already, running along the balcony towards the head of the stairs, pulling me behind her.

Down in the courtyard two of our servant girls were lying on the ground, their legs and arms twisted. They were as still as bundles of rags. I couldn't understand why, but Amma didn't give me time to look. She had thrown me up on to her back and was running low to the ground, bent over, so that I had to cling to her like a monkey. I looked over my shoulder. The last sight of my old home was of

Yetemegnu hurling bundles down from the balcony into the courtyard below, screaming fruitlessly for a servant to come and help her.

Amma stopped running when we came to the thorn fence that ran round the huts of the European prisoners. She faltered, as if the desperate energy that had driven her here had deserted her. She stood staring about her, lost.

I slid off her back.

'Is this it? The prison enclosure? Where's Mr Rassam's house?'

I tugged at her hand and we ran towards the largest of the huts. At any other time I would have been proud to be the one to show her the way, but I was so frightened of the shells exploding all around us that I felt only impatient with her.

'In here!' I said, pushing at the unlocked door of Mr Rassam's house. 'Get in, Amma. Quick!'

The last time I had been at that house, I had watched through the door as Mr Rassam, Dr Blanc and some of the other prisoners sat at the table in the middle of the round room, dealing out cards on to the cloth, their chained legs hidden by its white folds, while their Indian servants stood by, waiting for instructions. I think I half expected them still to be there. I wanted Mr Rassam to stand up and look concerned and assure us that he would look after us, that everything would be all right.

'Where's Mr Rassam?' I said indignantly.

'Your father released them all. They're with the British now – all the European prisoners,' Amma said bitterly. 'If only he'd done it months ago.'

'Then who's going to look after us?' I said furiously. 'Mr Rassam *ought* to be here! We *need* him!'

Amma didn't bother to answer. She was looking round the little house. It seemed different now that it was empty. The books and papers, the dishes, the washstand, the boots and dress uniforms had all gone. Only the large furniture was left – the table and some chairs.

I darted across to the inner room, where there was only one small window. The dim light there seemed to offer a little more protection.

'Amma, come on. Amma!'

I heard voices and running feet and dived under the bare frame of Mr Rassam's bed, pushing myself in as far as I could until I was crammed up against the wall. But then I recognized Yetemegnu's voice, and Gebre's.

'What's happening?' Amma's voice cracked with anxiety. No one answered.

'Listen! The shelling's stopped! Is it over? Have they given up? Where's the King?'

I heard the thump of bundles being thrown to the floor.

'He's holding them beyond the lower gate,' panted Yetemegnu. 'They're trying to break through.'

'They won't do it,' Amma said defiantly. 'The path's too narrow. Theodore can defend it easily with a few good men.'

'A few good men?' Yetemegnu's voice was rising and I thought she was about to go off into hysterics again. 'There are only ten men left with him. Everyone else is either dead or they've run away. The *ferenjis* will break through any time now!' Her breath was coming in rasping gasps. 'Oh God, save us! Oh God, what will happen to us?'

'You know what will happen to us,' Amma snapped at her. 'A victorious army? The King's women? We've got to hide. Get into the inner room. Alamayu's there. Gebre! Where's he gone? Gebre?'

'*Abet, Itege?*' came Gebre's shaky voice.

'Come inside! Get into the house and bolt the door. We must make them think the place is empty.'

The bed above me creaked as the bulk of Yetemegnu plumped down on it. She was rocking to and fro. I heard Gebre call out, 'The bolts are on the outside, *Itege*. We can't lock ourselves in.'

The strip of light which I could see from my corner under the bed was intensified to a sudden brilliant flash. I wanted to scream, but I could do no more than whimper.

'Lightning,' Amma said. 'God has sent us another storm.'

Then I heard her sit down beside Yetemegnu and begin to mumble prayers.

I knew nothing, of course, of what was happening outside, of the storming of Magdala by the British, of what Father was doing, but his fate has been described so often that I can see it in my mind's eye as clearly as if I'd witnessed it myself.

Yetemegnu had been right. Only a handful of men had stayed with him to the end. They had rolled boulders behind the lower gate, blocking it shut, but the British had good tools and many soldiers. They worked away at the gates with crowbars till they had prised them open, and began to clear away the boulders, while others climbed up the cliff and burst out above it, firing as they came.

Only five of our people survived the run up that steep path to the inner gate. Father pushed them all ahead of him, taking the greatest risk himself.

'Run!' he shouted to them. 'I free you from my service. Save yourselves! But they'll never take me alive!'

And he pulled his pistol out of his belt.

We heard many shots as we hid in Mr Rassam's house, but I don't know if we heard that fatal one. There was so much noise, so many shouts and bangs and running feet, that I put my hands over my ears, leaned on my knees and elbows and rocked backwards and forwards in my dark corner under Mr Rassam's bed. I think I was whispering, 'Father, come and find me. Father, make me safe,' but I don't remember now.

When at last I crawled out from under the bed, hands seized me. I kicked and struggled, but it was only Yetemegnu who held me. My bare heels sunk into her soft flesh. She passed me to Amma, who was still praying.

I curled my arms around Amma, and she pressed me so tightly against her chest that I could hardly breathe.

We were right to be so frightened. Men came, as she knew they would. There were three of them. I heard them shouting in English at the entrance to the house. Then came the grating sound as the bolts on the outside, which Gebre must have drawn across before he ran away to hide, were shot back. The three of us sat, trembling, on the bed, Amma and Yetemegnu trying to hide themselves under their *shammas*.

They shouted words, but what I remember is cries like animals make, braying, hooting, cackling, triumphant. They smelled of sweat and excitement. Their red faces were streaked with dirt, their pale eyes fierce and staring. One grabbed hold of Amma's arm, while another wrenched me away from her and threw me down on the bed. The third was yanking Yetemegnu to her feet. I know I fought them. I kicked and bit and struggled as much as I could. I like to think that I gave Amma the few precious seconds we needed.

Just in time there was a shout from the door. Another soldier ran in, and behind him, out of breath and moving more slowly, was Mr Rassam.

The new soldier (an officer) began screaming at our attackers. They dropped Amma and Yetemegnu at once, as if they were too hot, and to my surprise shuffled into a line, stamped their feet and saluted. Then they left the house.

Yetemegnu had fallen back on to the bed and was crying, but Amma stood up and tried to pull her *shamma* over her head and shoulders, from where the soldiers had ripped it away. The officer looked away from her, then backed politely out to stand by the door.

'My dear lady! Your Highness!' Mr Rassam was saying in Amharic. 'How very dreadful. Are you hurt? I wouldn't for the world have had this happen to you.'

'You came in time,' Amma said, holding her *shamma* close round her face. 'Thank you, Mr Rassam.' I've seen many queens and princesses since those days, but none have matched Amma's courage and dignity. 'Kindly tell me what is happening. Where's my husband?'

He bowed and pointed to one of the chairs beside the table. She took the hint, and sat down.

'He is gone,' he said gently. 'And by his own hand. He was courageous to the last.'

Amma only nodded.

I didn't understand what was happening.

'Please, Mr Rassam, what do you mean?' I said, pulling at his sleeve. 'Is Father all right? I want to see him.'

'Be quiet, Alamayu,' said Amma. 'Mr Rassam, what will happen to us now?'

'I assure you, madam, you will not be insulted again. A heavy guard is to be placed around the enclosure, and outside this house. It would be best for you to remain here for tonight, until arrangements can be made for your future. I will do everything possible to ensure your comfort. A British colonel – I think his name is Merewether – will call on you tomorrow to learn your wishes. In the meantime my servants will see that you are supplied with anything you need.'

'Thank you, but I have my own servants.'

He coughed delicately.

'If they can be found, Your Highness. Most of your people have fled.'

I couldn't stay quiet any longer.

'But where is Father, Mr Rassam? I want to see him! Take me to him now!'

The British carried my father's body away from the place where he had died before their soldiers could cut off any more pieces of his hair and clothes to take away as souvenirs. They laid him in the empty house of another European prisoner, near to Mr Rassam's.

I had to see him for myself. I had to understand

what had happened to him.

The European prisoners' enclosure had filled up by now. Everyone on Magdala had, like us, decided to take refuge there. Inside the thorn fence there was hardly room to move, and the air was filled with a terrible noise of donkeys braying, and people shouting to each other or wailing in grief.

The English officer had put several soldiers outside Mr Rassam's house to guard us. At first they wouldn't let anyone in, not even Abebech, who had been hiding during the storming of Magdala in the grain store of our old house, or Gebre, who had reappeared at last, looking a little ashamed at having deserted us just when we had needed him most. Luckily Mr Rassam came by again and told the soldiers he could let our people in. He said that Amma could receive visits from priests and other people if she wanted to. They soon came.

Everyone was too busy to notice me, so I slipped outside the house and found Gebre, who had rescued another load of bundles from our old home. The English soldiers were raiding it, and most of our belongings had already been stolen.

'I want to see Father,' I said to him. 'Take me to see him.'

'I can't do that, Prince. You know that His Majesty is dead.'

'I want to see him.'

'I'm sorry.'

I felt a dreadful misery wash over me. An awful dread. Out of my mouth came a cry louder than the sounds of grief around us.

Gebre crouched down so that his face was no higher than mine.

'I told you, my darling. The Emperor is dead. God has taken him.'

'I don't believe you!' I wailed. 'Why doesn't anyone tell me the truth?'

He looked at me for a long moment. Then he stood up and without another word held out his hand. I put mine into his, and together we pushed through the mass of people, climbing over sacks and bundles and ducking under the heads of mules.

More English soldiers were standing outside one of the foreigners' huts. They looked very tall to me. They stood stiffly, and as straight as tree trunks in their scarlet jackets. Without saying anything, they lowered the rifles they were holding across the doorway to stop us going inside.

'This is the King's son,' Gebre said. 'He wants to see his father.'

They didn't understand, of course.

'Theodore son,' Gebre said slowly.

The soldiers weren't even looking at us. They had fixed their eyes on a distant point, deliberately ignoring us, as if we were lice, as if we were too insignificant to attract their attention. It was my first experience of the imperial British stare, and it sent a shiver through me.

Dr Blanc came past at that moment and saw us standing helplessly there. He wasn't like Mr Rassam. He had never learned our language well, but he understood what we wanted.

I sensed a change in him. He had always been kind and respectful to me. After all, his life had been in my father's hands, and I suppose he had been very afraid. Now his chains had been struck off and he was free. He and his people had become our masters.

I didn't understand all that at the time, but I saw strange things in his face. Looking back, I'm not sure if he was feeling pity for me or contempt.

He spoke to the soldiers, who lowered their rifles and let us into the hut.

Father lay on a low table, only he wasn't there at all. Even though I was a child, I had seen death many times. I recognized it now. I knew at once that he had gone.

His face looked thinner. His hair was untidy and escaping from its plaits. There was a black burn mark by his mouth, but he seemed to be almost smiling.

I could see that he wasn't angry any more. He was in his soft, gentle mood. If he had come alive again at that moment, he might even have wanted to play with me.

People were singing outside the door, and then a crowd of priests came in. They had tied their *shammas* in the respectful way, to show that they were in the presence of the King. They moved round the table quietly, murmuring prayers.

I suddenly didn't want to see any more. I flung myself at Gebre, clutching him tightly round the waist.

'*Aisu*,' he said, using our word of comfort. 'He's at peace now. Come away. Let's go.'

Colonel Merewether came to us the next day, as Mr Rassam had promised. I didn't listen to all that went on. I pestered Gebre to take me home to our proper house, but he kept making excuses, and at last he became impatient with me and told me that I couldn't leave the *ferenji* enclosure because the British soldiers were all over Magdala, and they were drunk and stealing everything. He was sorry when he saw he had frightened me, and put me on his knee and started telling me stories, the ones I liked, about the clever fox and the cunning baboon.

What was strange to me that day was the change that had come over both Amma and Yetemegnu. Amma had lost all the fiery energy she had had the day before. She lay all day on Mr Rassam's bed, coughing, and when Colonel Merewether came she could hardly drag herself to sit up against the bolster.

Yetemegnu had completely got over her fright. She smiled at everyone, twitched her *shamma*, and spoke softly in her oily voice, looking up with her head on one side at the soldiers who came to call.

All I understood in the end was that the three of us were to set off from Magdala with the British Army and the rescued *ferenji* prisoners, and that Yetemegnu would be leaving us after a while to return to her own people in the north. I didn't understand – how could I? – that we were starting on a great journey, one that would take me across deserts and seas and all the way to Britain.

Taking us down from Magdala to Selamge the next day was quite a complicated business. The lower gate had fallen in, and the narrow path was made even more dangerous with tumbled stone and boulders. The British had given us mules to carry the few bundles we'd rescued from our house before the looters got to it.

I couldn't understand why Amma wasn't getting any better. Her cough had become much worse and she seemed to have become quite feeble. Abebech and Gebre had to half carry her down the path, and once we were on the flat of Selamge they brought up a mule for her to ride. A troop of soldiers came with us. I was afraid they would attack Amma, as the others had done, but they were respectful, and one of them even picked me up to carry me over the most dangerous part of the path.

I went rigid with fright, but after a while, when I saw

that he didn't mean to hurt me, I had a good look at the man and what he was wearing. It was easy, as my nose was inches from his collar. His chin was stuck all over with stiff red bristles and angry-looking pimples. His scarlet jacket looked hot and uncomfortable to me, the cloth too thick and scratchy. It smelled too, of old sweat and dirt. I dared to put out my hand to touch one of the bright metal buttons that ran down the front of the jacket.

He put me down when we reached the bottom of the track. I was glad. I felt safer on my own two feet. He had not been comfortably bare foot, like our people always were, and the soles of his leather boots had slipped and skidded on the loose stones.

The soldiers led us to Mr Rassam's tent. It was a big one, which he had brought from Egypt. He had kept it rolled up with his other baggage during his long imprisonment, and I had never seen it before. The inside was covered with nice patterns cut from coloured cloth, and he had covered the floor with the carpets Father had given him. It was a good place to be, and I ran about, looking at everything. I tried to get Amma to look too, but she had sunk down straight away on to some cushions. Abebech was hovering over her and shooed me away.

Amma stirred a bit when Mr Rassam came in, and tried to sit up to thank him for looking after us, but the movement made her cough.

'You are safe now, *Itege,*' he kept saying. 'No one will

harm you. General Napier himself has promised that you will receive every mark of respect and all the comfort we can offer.'

'I don't doubt it, Mr Rassam,' she said.

I think he was waiting for her to smile, but when she didn't he said again, 'You're quite safe now.'

'My whole life has been miserable!' she burst out suddenly, startling him and me. 'Ever since I was a child! The only happiness I can look forward to now is to be with my Saviour in heaven!'

I hated it when she said things like that. I ran outside and found Gebre, and I made him take me to look at the elephants.

There were Indian men in charge of the elephants, and I saw, now that I was right in the middle of the British Army, that many of the soldiers were darker-skinned than the *ferenjis*. They were all from India, I think. Everyone was kind to me. They let me go right up to the elephants and run my hands over their rough, wrinkled sides.

I chattered about them to Gebre all the way back to our tent.

'Did you see how hairy they are, Gebre? Did you see the pink inside their trunks?'

Going back into Mr Rassam's tent felt like going home. It wasn't so different from our big room in the King's House in Magdala. Amma was lying on cushions like ours, Yetemegnu's maid was plaiting her hair, one of our cooks, who had crept out of hiding to join us again, was preparing our supper, and the smells of woodsmoke and frying lamb wafted in from his cooking fire behind the tent, as it had always done in the King's House.

'We saw the elephants, Amma!' I said to her, hopping up and down in front of her and trying to make her look at me. 'The man – he's called a mahout – said he'd let me ride on one tomorrow. They're so big, and when they flap their ears . . .'

Her coughing interrupted me, and Gebre came up and took me away.

I can't bear to go on remembering all that just now. I want to fix my mind on something else. The trouble is that all I can think of is Ivor Carson.

Carson was a senior boy here at Rugby last year who was like a god to most of the school. Everyone thought he was very handsome, with his fair curly hair and blue eyes. He was the captain of the school Rugby football team, and every time he went out to the playing field, younger boys followed him and stood on the sidelines to watch. They cheered whenever he tackled someone or picked up the ball to run with it.

I never admired Carson like the other boys did, but I wouldn't have dared to say so. I thought they were silly for believing in him so wholeheartedly. When you put your trust in people, when you let your guard down and start to love them, you put yourself in danger. I've learned that in the end they'll always let you down. Anyway, I knew almost from the start that Carson didn't deserve any of the admiration he was given.

As I lie here, Carson's handsome, cruel face is right there in front of me.

The first time he singled me out was not long after I came to Rugby. He was coming off the football field after scoring a triumphant try, covered in mud but basking in glory too.

'Our Abyssinian prince,' he said, looking down at me. (Did I say that he was very tall?) 'How do you say your name?'

'A-lem-ai-you,' I said slowly. I was used to doing that for people.

Other boys in my form were running up to see what was

going on. Carson always had the power to draw them. I waited nervously. Something about him made me feel anxious.

'My father fought in the Abyssinia Campaign,' Carson said. 'He's a brigadier in the Bengal Lancers.'

The others looked at him admiringly. I waited nervously, not knowing what to expect.

'He told me that he had never, in all his years in the Lancers, seen such courage as the Abyssinian savages showed in their charge at Magdala. "Magnificent," he called them. You should be proud, Alamayu.'

'I am, Carson.'

'If we hadn't had modern rifles, it would have been a fairer fight, my old man said. But no bunch of ragged natives could beat a well-trained British Army with Snider rifles. Your people had only the most primitive weapons, you know.'

'I do know,' I managed to say.

To my horror I felt tears well up in my eyes. I knew that I must never, ever, let anyone see me cry. I swallowed hard.

Carson was actually patting me on the shoulder.

'I suppose you didn't see the battle, did you?'

There was such a crowd around us now and my feelings were choking me so completely that I could hardly speak.

'I heard the King my father give the order,' I said unwillingly. 'I . . . I was only small then. My . . . my servant carried me away when the cannon opened up.'

He was waiting for me to go on, but I couldn't have said another word.

'Well,' he said. 'Well.' He paused. 'I hope you're happy here, Al- what was it again? Ah yes, Alamayu. I hope you realize how generous we British are to our fallen enemies? We hold no grudge against your father, you know.'

The tone of his voice was smooth and kind, but a bolt of rage shot through me, taking my breath away. I knew better than to show it.

'I know that, Carson,' I said stiffly. 'Her Majesty has been a good friend to me.'

There was a slight intake of breath all around me. I don't usually speak about Queen Victoria. It starts off too many tiresome questions. In any case, princes and queens shouldn't gossip about each other. As soon as I'd spoken, I wished I'd said something else.

Even Carson was looking impressed.

'You've met her, haven't you? You've actually been to her house on the Isle of Wight? What did she say to—'

Luckily the clock chimed at that moment. The clock is the voice of command at Rugby. You have to do what it says at once. As soon as they heard the first stroke, the crowd of boys ran off. They made me think of the clouds of minnows in the stream, which Beetle scatters when he throws a pebble in among them.

The British stole everything from us after the fall of Magdala. Perhaps an Abyssinian army would have done the same thing, but not in the orderly, calculated British way. They brought my nation's wealth down from the heights of Magdala to the flat ground of Selamge under an armed guard, where an expert from the British Museum, sent specially from London, could take his pick.

They laid our treasures out on the ground. Their loot covered an area the size of a football pitch. They spread Father's finest carpets across the bare grass and on top of them they piled sacred things from our churches: silver goblets and cups, gold crosses, canopies, vestments, paintings, illustrated Bibles and other holy books. They took the precious icon that had always hung above Father's bed. They took his crowns, his shield, his swords, his guns and his ornamental saddles. They took Amma's jewellery and her embroidered dresses and silk cushions. They took everything that they could carry.

Emperor Theodore's cross

Why didn't I cry out when they pawed over our belongings and sold them in their auction? Why didn't I run between their long, tight-trousered legs and snatch up Father's jewelled dagger, or his golden bracelet, or Hamra's decorated bridle?

I hate to remember how I stayed inside Mr Rassam's tent all that day, how I looked out through the flaps, barely noticing the glittering plunder as they sold it among themselves, wanting only for Gebre to take me back to the mahouts so that I could ride on an elephant. But Gebre wouldn't leave the tent, and I was too scared to go out on my own. I was confused by the strange antics of the *ferenji* soldiers, the way they shouted to each other in rude, loud voices, which must have carried for miles in the still mountain air. I jumped with fright every time a bugle was blown. I was scared of the long-barrelled guns still pointing up towards Magdala, and of the gunners who lounged around them. But how can I regret those hours I spent close to Amma? If only one of them, half of one of them, would come again.

Samuel, Mr Rassam's Abyssinian servant, was the one who organized everything. The next morning it was Samuel who woke Gebre (who had slept across the doorway of our tent to guard us) and told him to get us packed up because the men were already waiting to take down the tent. I was the first to jump up. I wriggled out from under the *shamma* that had covered me during the cold night.

'Are we going home today?' I asked Samuel. 'I really want to go home.'

He looked perplexed and turned to Gebre, who was still yawning and rubbing his eyes.

'Hasn't anyone explained to him? Doesn't he know what's happening?'

'I have told him, *Ato* Samuel,' said Gebre respectfully, 'again and again, but he doesn't wish to understand.'

Our few possessions were soon removed from Mr Rassam's tent, and when Samuel and the other servants lowered the poles the canvas billowed out as it collapsed on to the ground with a sighing sound. Even the illusion of being at home sank to nothing with it.

Samuel and Gebre didn't seem to be afraid of the British soldiers. They went about their tasks without once looking over their shoulders. They made me feel less frightened too.

I stood blinking in the bright morning sunshine. Dr Blanc had been summoned to see to Amma, who had hardly opened her eyes. She lay on a wooden frame that some soldiers had brought up for her. It had hoops over it, and a cloth to cover them that protected her from the sun and people's stares. They called it a 'dooley'. Inside it was like a little long tent. I pushed my head into it and tried to make her watch how the British soldiers were all lining up and how their officers were marching around, each one with a stick held tight under his arm, but she only moaned when a shaft of sunlight shone on her face and turned her head away. I was offended that she didn't want to talk to me.

Dr Blanc came. He pulled aside the dooley's cover and made Amma drink something out of a bottle. It must have tasted nasty, because she screwed up her face and coughed.

I went on watching while all around me tents were disappearing into bundles and soldiers were strapping their masses of equipment on to mules. Some of them had taken off their shirts and jackets and they were working with their skin bared to the sun. I couldn't stop staring at their red shining backs, which looked raw, as if they had been peeled. I thought they were indecent.

Gebre brought up a black mule.

'It's for you to ride,' he said, looking pleased.

It was the right thing for me, because a mule is the correct mount for a prince, but then I saw that something was wrong.

'I won't ride that thing,' I said loudly. 'It doesn't have a velvet saddlecloth, or a royal saddle.'

I don't know why, but the plain saddle and the lack of an ornamental cloth struck me as dreadful, and I wanted to cry.

Gebre understood. At least I think he did. He started saying something, but then Yetemegnu set up a screech, complaining about the mule she had been given to ride, and I didn't want to be like her, so I swallowed the tears that had sprouted in my eyes. After that Gebre changed towards me a little bit. He became less like a servant and more like an older brother. I didn't notice it at first.

I had seen our Abyssinian armies on the move. I had watched Father riding out in front, his pages following him, carrying his shield, his gun and his telescope. I had seen his cavalry swinging into line behind him, and I had cheered our thousands of foot soldiers, their muskets and spears across their shoulders, following on at a fast trot. I had never bothered to look at the thousands more who followed behind, men and women, cooks and water carriers and muleteers.

It was different with the British. I was impressed by the way they did things, so strictly and with such discipline. Everyone seemed to have something to do, and they performed their tasks with astonishing speed.

I couldn't have put the feeling into words, but from that moment on I suppose I began to understand that I had lost my position in the world. The British Army moved like a well-oiled machine, making me feel as unimportant as a single spoke in one of the wheels of the big guns the men were taking apart. I had been used to see respect and even awe in the eyes of everyone I had met, but I was no longer the precious son of a feared and powerful king. I was the child of a man and a nation defeated.

I let Gebre lift me on to my mule when Samuel came running to tell us that it was time for our small group to set off. We were to ride near the head of the long procession of men and animals that was waiting to wind down the steep path from Selamge into the gorge below. Gebre walked ahead, holding my mule by the bridle. Amma's dooley came behind me, and then came Yetemegnu, still grumbling, on her mule. I think I looked round to see if Amma was all right. I hope I did. At any rate, I remember how the dooley swayed on the shoulders of the bearers carrying it, and how the curtains flapped.

We had gone all the way down into the gorge and were riding up the steep path on the far side when sudden explosions sent me cowering down in my saddle. I felt as if the breath was being pressed out of my body.

'Gebre,' I shouted, 'make them stop it!'

My mule was startled by the noise. He jolted to a stop, tossed his head and began to kick out with his hind hoofs. Gebre didn't even look at me. His eyes were fixed on Magdala behind us, and his mouth had fallen open. The bearers of Amma's dooley and the soldiers escorting us had halted too. They were gasping, and sucking the air in between their teeth.

At last I did dare to swivel my head for a moment, to take one quick look at Magdala. It only needed a second for the terrible sight to be printed on my eyes. Flames were shooting up into the sky, and new explosions were sending up showers of sparks.

'Is our house burning too?' I cried out in a panic.

The destruction of Magdala

'Of course it is, you silly child,' Yetemegnu called in a rough voice. She had never spoken to me like that before. 'Now that our Lord the King is dead, the whole of Abyssinia might as well go up in flames.'

It's Sunday today, and just now I heard the singing from the chapel where the fellows have all gone for the service. I don't like to admit it, but it made me cry. I would never cry if I was well, but now I don't seem able to stop the tears sliding out from under my eyelids and creeping down my cheeks. It's not that the music made me feel sad. It's just that it made me feel.

I've been trying to remember the sounds of our Abyssinian music – the tinkling of the priests' silver sistra, the mournful tunes of our stringed instruments and the wild rush of notes from our nose flutes, but I can't any longer hear in my head the sounds they made.

If I can't remember the music of the priests, I can hear all too clearly the singing of the British Army. There's one tune that refuses to go out of my head. The troops sang it as the long cavalcade of men and beasts came in at the end of each day to the place where camp would be made for the night.

> *'Here we are again!*
> *Happy as can be.*
> *All good pals*
> *In jolly good company.'*

I can't get that silly tune out of my head. It beats a tattoo in my ears.

> *Da-di-da-di-da*
> *Da-di-da . . .*

And on and on.

I was used to the freezing cold of early mornings in Magdala and I was used to the hot sun of midday. I was used to travelling long distances and not complaining if I was hungry. I was used to being told that I was a prince and that I must never show fear, or give way to tears, or let anyone sense that I felt weak.

But that terrible journey away from Magdala across the harsh mountains and through the wild valleys of Abyssinia was dreadfully weary and long to me. Every evening, when at last we halted and the soldiers rushed to make camp, my legs were stiff and sore with climbing up paths too steep for riding, and my hands ached from holding the reins when the mule needed to go slow on the downward slopes.

I can still hear the sounds of that army on the move: the clatter of hoofs on the loose stones of the paths, the curses of men coaxing frightened animals along the narrow sides of sheer cliffs, the cries of the mahouts to their elephants, the whistles of the Naval Brigade, the barking shouts of officers, the penetrating bugle calls with their own language of commands, and in the sky above us, wheeling above the peaks or perching aloft on rocky outcrops, the kites and eagles sending out their long drawn-out mournful cries.

The first blast of the bugle every day was the one I learned first. They called it reveille, and it often rang out long before dawn. Amma, Yetemegnu and I were travelling close to the chief, Sir Robert Napier himself, and everything around him was done neatly and quickly. Gebre never ceased to be amazed.

'You can see a row of white tents one minute, hundreds of them,' he would say admiringly, 'and you close your eyes just for a blink, and when you open them again, they've all disappeared.'

There were eight bearers to carry Amma's dooley. Abebech walked beside her, of course. Sir Robert had given Amma a water carrier and a medical attendant, along with a dozen soldiers to escort her. He treated her (and Yetemegnu too, I suppose) like a queen. I don't think even Father would have looked after her better.

Every night, when we arrived at the camping site, servants would hurry to put up Mr Rassam's tent for us, and the illusion of a kind of home would comfort me.

I'm ashamed to say that I was angry with Amma all those evenings for not talking to me or telling me stories like she used to do in Magdala. I wish I could say I had not been.

In the evenings, after the day's march, people would walk around the camp visiting each other, but hardly anyone came to see us. Many Abyssinians were travelling with the British Army until they could safely branch off to their own homes, but few of them called on Amma any more. Mr Rassam would stop and enquire after her whenever he went past, but he seldom came inside. General Napier's own doctor often came to see her. He used to hold her wrist, which puzzled me, and he'd look serious and give her some medicine, then silently go out again. I liked him better than Dr Blanc.

A few days after we left Magdala, I began to notice a strange person who was always going in and out of Sir Robert's tent. He seemed to be respected by everyone, but I wanted to laugh every time I caught sight of him.

He was very tall – the tallest person I had ever seen – and his hair was actually red. I was amazed to see such a colour on a person's head before, and it made me want to stare at him. This man had bright blue eyes. He wore round spectacles with thick glass in them, but the glass was usually so smeared that it was hard to see his eyes at all unless he took his spectacles off.

It was his clothes that were really odd. Instead of the scarlet jacket and blue trousers which the other *ferenji* soldiers wore, he wandered about in a strange collection of things, some Abyssinian, some English. A red scarf was tied round his head and the lion-skin cape of a nobleman round his neck, with one of our white *shammas* over his shoulders. Underneath was a proper tunic, like Father's, but below it you could see his army-uniform blue trousers and boots.

I wanted to ask Mr Rassam about the man, but I didn't dare. My princely confidence was ebbing away from me. I was afraid of looking ignorant and making a fool of myself. I stayed close to our people.

Captain Speedy

It was Gebre who found things out for me.

'That strange man, Prince, he is called Captain Speedy. He knew His Majesty, your father. He visited him years ago. *Jan Hoy* liked him, I think. He called him Basha Felika.'

(*Basha* means 'captain' in my language, and *Felika* means 'speedy'.)

'Why does he look so funny?' I asked Gebre.

'He isn't funny. He likes to wear our clothes. He's a good man, everyone says. He talks in Amharic really well.'

'But it's silly to wear shoes,' I objected. 'It shows he's not a real man.'

'Oh, Basha Felika is a real man. When your father called for a champion to fight him in single combat, Basha Felika pleaded to be the one, but Chief Napier wouldn't let him.'

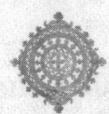

One dark night, after a long day's march, we were all exhausted. It had rained that morning. I had been wet through, and though my clothes had nearly dried in the sun once it had risen, I hadn't shaken off the chill. Amma seemed sicklier than ever and hardly swallowed a mouthful of the food Abebech pressed on her.

It was a bitterly cold night. We couldn't have a fire in our tent, of course, but Gebre found a brazier filled with some glowing charcoal from somewhere and brought it in to us. He set it down near Amma, who turned her head gratefully towards the heat, and I squatted down beside her and stretched out my hands to warm my frozen fingers.

I was sleepy and was about to crawl into my usual place on a rug near Amma, when I heard voices speaking in English at the door. Then came a polite cough.

Gebre, who was squatting, yawning, just inside the closed tent flaps, jumped up and peered out.

'*Abet?* Who is it?'

'Rassam. I'm here with Captain Speedy. The Queen has asked to see him.'

'*Ishi.* Wait here, please.'

Abebech had stood up from her usual place by Amma's side. 'Not now. The Queen is too sick. Tomorrow.'

Amma was struggling to lift her head. 'Who is it? What do they want?'

'Mr Rassam, *Itege.* With another *ferenji.*'

'Let them come in.'

Gebre lifted the flap. Outside, the moon had risen and the whole world shone silver and grey. I suppose the inside of the tent must have seemed pitch dark in contrast to that unearthly light. At any rate, although Mr Rassam came in easily enough, Captain Speedy, who entered after him, seemed as clumsy as a blind man. He failed to bend down low enough and knocked his head on the tent rail, nearly losing his balance. Once he had lurched inside, he trod on Yetemegnu, who was lying rolled in her *shamma*, snoring, by the tent wall. She sat up with a yelp and startled him so much that he lunged across the carpeted floor. He was so huge that I was afraid he would blunder into the tent pole and bring it all crashing down.

I couldn't help giggling. I nearly laughed out loud. I could tell at once that I need not be afraid of Captain Speedy, or Basha Felika, as I would call him, even though he was such a giant and looked so strange. In fact, I think I liked him from that very moment.

I ran up and took hold of his hand to stop him stumbling again. His hand was like a paw, so huge that it swallowed mine up completely, but it was gentle too. He steadied himself, and when he was ready I led him over to where Amma lay.

Even in the dim light from the brazier, I could see that she was smiling.

'Can you see me now, Basha Felika?'

'Yes. I – I'm sorry, Your Majesty. So clumsy . . .'

'You had my message? You came. Thank you.'

I opened my eyes at that. Amma knew this strange man? She had invited him to come?

He knelt down beside her.

'I am sorry, *Itege*, to see that you are unwell.'

He spoke Amharic much better than Dr Blanc, but not as well as Mr Rassam.

'You see how I am,' she said. 'It won't be much longer.'

'Surely, madam, God will spare . . .'

She lifted a hand, and dropped it again as if the effort was too much. 'I don't wish for it. If I could live, it would only be for the sake of Alamayu.'

Basha Felika seemed embarrassed, but he looked round, saw me and smiled. 'He has grown so much since I last saw him. I would hardly have recognized him.'

I gaped at him. Had this extraordinary man known me before?

He let out a rumbling laugh. 'This young rascal made me sit him on my horse, and he cried when I tried to take him off.'

It was the sound of that laugh that brought him back to me. I *had* seen this man before, with Father. He *had* put me up on his great horse. I had been a bit scared, but I had liked it too.

Amma gave a tiny shake of her head. She seemed to be filled with a sense of purpose. I think she was afraid that she would run out of strength before she could finish what she wanted to do.

'Basha Felika,' she said, fixing her eyes intently on him, 'Mr Rassam has been good to us, but he is not returning directly to England with the forces. Colonel Merewether has been kind too, but he cannot speak Amharic, and I . . . I don't know him.'

A coughing fit interrupted her. She had been trying to raise her head but gave up. Abebech dabbed at the side of her mouth with a cloth, and when she took it away I saw a dark stain on it.

'You're a good man,' Amma went on. 'The King thought well of you. You understand our language and our customs.'

She looked past Basha Felika at Abebech and gave a tiny nod. Abebech leaned behind her and picked up the worn Bible which Amma kept beside her at all times.

'Give me your hand, Basha Felika.'

I think she knew he would obey her. Everyone always did. He could have crushed Amma's long slender fingers like twigs in his powerful grasp, but he touched them as delicately as if they were butterflies' wings.

'Here, lay your hand on my Bible.'

He did so. She laid hers on top of his.

'What is it you want, *Itege*?'

She spoke in a desperate rush. 'That you'll care for my son. That you'll protect him. Be a father to him. He's going to need you. His . . . His need will be very great.'

He didn't hesitate. Behind the thick glass of Basha Felika's spectacles I could see that his eyes were wet.

'I swear this to you solemnly, *Itege*. On the Bible. I will be a father to him.'

She let out a great sigh, then moved her eyes to me. 'Come here, Alamayu.'

I crept close. I knew that something momentous was happening. I didn't understand what it was.

'You're to obey Basha Felika. He'll be like a father to you now.'

The glow from the charcoal was dying down and it was almost completely dark in the tent. I heard a scraping sound behind me, and light flickered round the cloth walls. Mr Rassam had lit a candle. Now he brought it over to us.

'There's something else, Basha Felika,' Amma said. 'Swear again, that you will make sure that Alamayu is brought up in the Christian religion. That he remains faithful to Christ.'

Basha Felika was very still. 'I swear.'

Abebech came forward and lifted his great hand off the Bible. It had been resting on Amma's chest and the weight must have been tiring for her.

'You have – relieved me – of a terrible anxiety,' Amma whispered. 'Come back tomorrow, Basha Felika. I'll tell you more about Alamayu tomorrow.'

Outside my window I can hear the clatter of boots on the flagstones of the quad as the boys line up to go into chapel for morning prayers. It makes me feel lonely to hear them down there, doing all the usual things without me.

Our chapel at Rugby is so new that the dust left by the stonemasons hangs in the air and you can still smell the freshly sawn wood of the pews. We have to go into the chapel every morning for prayers, and twice on Sundays. I like it when the bell rings to call us. I join the long line of boys trooping in through the doors, knowing that no one can try to get inside my head for a while.

The chapel is long and the painted ceiling is very high. It's quite dim inside because of the coloured glass in the windows. When the sun shines through them, patterns of red, blue and green colour the faces of the boys, who sit facing each other down the length of the nave.

Recently, when I've been in the chapel, I've turned my head to look at the picture made out of glass in the big east window above the altar. It shows the Virgin Mary, with Jesus on her knee. She sits like a queen, holding her baby son, with important people standing all around her or kneeling at her feet.

The chapel at Rugby School

When I first came to Rugby I couldn't bear that picture of glowing glass. I preferred to stare at the complicated patterns made by the orange bricks and cream-coloured stones on the opposite wall. Staring at them, I would try to block out Dr Jex-Blake's long sermons as I waited for the music to begin.

The Virgin isn't looking at the baby Jesus, but her arm encircles him and she seems to lean into him in a loving sort of way. I was afraid that Amma had never held me like that. I used to hate her sometimes for giving me away to Basha Felika. I used to think that she could have gone on living if she'd wanted to, that she chose to die.

I don't feel angry with Amma any more. I know now that she did her best for me. It was good, what she did. If only Basha Felika hadn't . . .

I won't let myself go down another angry road. I don't need to count the squares on the mosaics any more either. I can look at the Virgin and her child and take their love into myself.

I wish I could remember what Amma looked like, but her face has slipped away from me. All I can remember is the softness of her voice and the feel of her hand on mine.

There was no travelling the next day. The vast procession of men and guns and animals had halted. We all needed a rest. Even the elephants did. They had begun to look thin and dejected. Their trunks were drooping.

General Napier's doctor came to our tent in the morning, and I saw him shake his head and look grave after he had examined Amma. Mr Rassam kept sending Samuel with special food that *ferenjis* give to sick people, but Amma wouldn't touch it. Abebech wouldn't have let her, even if she'd wanted to. She sniffed at the bowls suspiciously and handed them back to Samuel. Amma would barely touch the food that our people cooked for her.

There was a storm that night. It was worse than the storm on the day of the battle. Inside our tent the flashes of lightning were bright enough to hurt our eyes, and it felt as if the thunder wasn't in the sky but exploding up from the ground beneath us.

The storm terrified me. It felt as if we were being fired at again, as if shells were landing all around us. I crept to Amma's bed on the cushions and pressed myself to her as close as I could, wanting her to turn and put her arms round me.

'Leave her to rest,' Abebech said, frowning at me, but Amma gave a tiny shake of her head and Abebech gave up and sat back on her heels. She was murmuring prayers and stopped every now and then to sigh.

'Amma,' I whispered, 'it's all right. You don't have to

give me to Basha Felika. I'm going to look after you. I won't run off any more in the way you don't like. Listen. I've had an idea. I know you can't speak at the moment, but if you need me in the night and I'm asleep, just pinch me. I'll wake up and start looking after you.'

She smiled a bit. I think she did.

I waited for a long time for her pinch. It never came.

I was the one who knew first.

'Abebech,' I whispered, 'I don't think she's breathing any more.'

The thunder was further away now, but a roll of it drowned my words.

'Abebech!' I cried, my voice sharp with fear.

I think Abebech had been dozing, but her head jerked up. She leaned forward and looked into Amma's face.

She flung her *shamma* over her head and began to wail loudly. People ran into the tent. I didn't see who they were. I didn't care. Gebre picked me up. I know that. I fought him. I bit and scratched him.

'She's asleep! Stop making such a noise! You'll wake her up! Put me down! Don't take me away!'

He didn't listen to me. He took me outside and ran with me to Basha Felika's tent. It was a small one, a simple officer's tent, hardly big enough for such a giant man. Basha Felika came out, blinking, at Gebre's call.

'Basha, the Queen is dead,' Gebre said, and passed me, like a bundle, into Basha Felika's huge embrace.

It seems hard to understand now, but I think I felt more indignant than anything else. I didn't try to fight Basha Felika as I had fought Gebre. For one thing, he was much too strong for me. For another, I didn't know him, and my strict training had taught me not to show feelings to strangers.

While Gebre had gone back to fetch my few things Basha Felika put me down on his bedroll, on which he had been resting. He squatted down beside me and took my hands in his.

'Don't be afraid,' he said. 'Don't be afraid.'

I wouldn't look at him. 'Please take me back to my tent. I wish to return to my mother.'

I expected him to refuse, but he surprised me by saying,

'In a little while, Prince. They have to . . . Let them do what they need to do first.'

Then I looked at him. 'Gebre is an ignorant slave. He said the Queen was dead. It isn't true, is it? Chief Napier's doctor is going to make her better.'

He dropped his head so that now I was looking straight into his thick hair, made even redder by the light of his candle.

'The doctor has done everything he can do. He told me

earlier today that there was . . . there was no . . . yes, Prince. She has gone to be with her Saviour in heaven.'

That made sense to me. I nodded. 'I know that. It's where she wanted to go. But does it mean that she can't come back from there?'

It was a silly question. Even as I asked it, I knew it.

He gently squeezed my hands. 'No one comes back from there.'

I swallowed. I couldn't think about it any more.

'Who's going to be in charge of the royal household then?' I asked. 'That other one?'

'You mean Queen Yetemegnu?'

'She's *not* a queen! Amma is the Queen!' The thump of anger in my voice surprised him.

He nodded.

'You're right. She's not a queen. And she will be returning to her own people tomorrow.'

'Then I'm in charge now, but I don't know what to do.'

I heard Gebre cough outside.

'It's Gebre. You can come in!' I called out.

Gebre had to duck low to come in under the tent roof, and the little space was crowded with the three of us inside. His arms were full of my few possessions, which he dropped on to Basha Felika's bedroll.

'If there's anything missing I can fetch it tomorrow,' he told Basha Felika. He didn't look at me.

I glared at him. 'What are they doing to Amma? I want

to go back. You must take me back now!'

'I can't, Prince. They're – they're preparing her.'

'What for?'

'They will . . . There will be a burial, a funeral, in the morning.'

I couldn't pretend any more. I understood then fully and finally that Amma was dead. I had seen many, many people put into the ground and the earth shovelled over them. I knew that it was the end. But I clung to the idea that she had not been buried yet.

'You must take me to her! I must see her!'

Basha Felika raised his eyebrows to Gebre, and after a long hesitation he gave a tiny nod. Basha Felika stood up as far as he could, stooping under the tent's low roof.

'Come on then,' he said, holding out his arms. 'I'll carry you.'

'I'm not a baby. I can walk,' I said.

Our tent wasn't far away. I started to run towards it, making the other two speed up to keep pace with me, but I slowed as I came near.

A crowd had gathered round the tent. All the Abyssinians who were travelling with the British Army had come to pay their respects to the Queen. The chiefs, their families, the grooms and other servants were crying out and beating their chests.

I tried to hold my head high. They saw me coming and parted to let me through, clicking their tongues

At the funeral of the Queen

and murmuring with sympathy.

Amma didn't look like herself any more. Abebech had laid her embroidered velvet cloak over her and wrapped something round her head.

I struggled to reach her, but Abebech held me back.

'Take that thing off her head,' I shouted, starting to cry. 'She doesn't like it.'

No one took any notice. A crowd of priests stood beside her body. They were swinging censers on silver chains, from which billowed up clouds of incense smoke. They were chanting in low, mournful tones.

Our own servants, Abebech and all the others, had picked up little bits and pieces that had belonged to Amma – a slipper, a scarf, a headrest, a wooden comb, a horn cup – and they were waving them in the air, chanting her name.

I couldn't see Yetemegnu at all. She had gone.

Amma was laid to rest properly, like the queen she was. The army was supposed to move off again at dawn that day, but the departure was delayed because of her funeral. A regimental band played the Dead March as they carried her body away to the church at Chelicut, nearby.

I don't think Amma would have wanted *ferenji* music at

her funeral. I don't think that band should have played. She would have wanted to hear only the cries of sorrow from our people and the chanting of our priests. She wouldn't have liked to be surrounded by white men and foreign voices. She would have wanted to see only her royal umbrella and her Bible held aloft, and the swaying crosses, and the scented smoke of incense billowing up from the swinging censers. She would have preferred her own warriors in their lion's-mane headdresses to run beside her coffin, rather than the ranks of men in scarlet jackets and white helmets marching in their orderly way.

The British thought they were doing the right thing. They knew they were burying a queen, but they didn't understand our ways.

I think God made Amma die in that place because it wasn't far from the church where her own grandfather had been buried. There was a noble tomb for him there, and the British took her to lie beside him.

The nights are the worst times here in the sickroom. The day nurse, Nurse Thomson, goes off and the night nurse comes. She's old and fat. She fusses over me too much, trying to make me take sips of water. Then she settles down in the chair at the foot of the bed and falls asleep straight away. Nothing wakes her up. If my blankets slip off, I'm too weak to lean out of bed and haul them up again. I just have to lie and shiver.

Sometimes I toss and turn most of the night, counting off the hours with the chimes of the clock. It's then that the worst and saddest memories come flooding back to me. I have to fight to keep them away. I try not to go back to Abyssinia during the night. I try to let my thoughts stay in Rugby.

After Amma died, I had no relatives to look after me. Amma's mother, my grandmother, still lived, but she was far away. Even if the British had been able to contact her, she wouldn't have been able to protect me. None of Amma's brothers wanted to take me. I suppose my father's shadow lay too heavily on me. The British had decided to take me to England, to Queen Victoria, and that was that.

Everything changed after Amma died. It wasn't just my situation that was different. Something had altered inside me. There was a stone where my heart had once been, a lump of fear, cold and heavy.

It wasn't Basha Felika who frightened me, or the soldiers who surrounded me with their swords and guns. It wasn't even the idea of going to England, a strange place which I couldn't begin to imagine. It was a nameless fear. An all-consuming dread.

Small things would bring on a fit of it. A shadow moving on a tent wall as someone passed outside would seem to me to be the shape of a demon. I would mistake the rumble of a gun carriage over rough ground for the growl of a lion. A flicker of lightning in the mountains behind us would look like the burst of a shell from a cannon's mouth.

But I was – I am – a prince. I knew that I shouldn't show my fear, except of course to Gebre, and, after a while, to Basha Felika. I trusted him. Perhaps it was because he was so big and strong. Or because he spoke Amharic and had known both my father and my mother. At any rate, he knew how to reassure me and comfort me.

As the long snake of men and animals wound down the narrow trails, further and further from Magdala, the heartlands of Abyssinia and the place where Amma was buried, I was undergoing the change that was to transform me. I was beginning the slow process of leaving my old self behind and turning into an English boy.

We were moving all the time down towards the sea. As we went our people drifted away from the protection of the British Army, disappearing silently in ones and twos along well-trodden paths to their old homes and families. By the time we came to the British base at Senafe, nearly all the Abyssianians had gone.

I didn't care about most of them, but I minded dreadfully about Abebech, and it still makes me catch my breath when I think of her. At Senafe she knelt down beside me, took my face in her hands and kissed me goodbye. She was only a slave woman, Amma's servant, but she had been my second mother. I knew her smell, and the softness of her arms holding me. I knew the roughness of her voice when she scolded me, and the kindness in it when she told me stories, or laughed at my little tricks, or brought me my favourite things to eat.

'I would have stayed with you forever, my darling,' she said, with tears running down her cheeks, 'but I don't dare go in a ship across the sea. I can't go to a *ferenji* land, where I don't know anyone.'

'You know me, Abebech.'

She pulled in her breath and let it out again in one of her huge sighs. 'God go with you, Alamayu. Pray to God as your blessed mother did. God will protect you. One day you'll come home to us, and they'll put a crown on your head. When they do, remember your old nurse Abebech.'

I seemed to belong to Basha Felika now, and I took to following him around the camp like a dog. I hadn't expected, though, that I would have to leave Mr Rassam's familiar tent, with its embroidered walls, its carpets and cushions, and the lingering smell of the oil which Abebech had used to dress Amma's hair. I only found out about it when I tried to go back inside and found Samuel there, arranging Mr Rassam's camp bed, and travelling washstand.

'You may leave,' I said to him. 'I wish to play in here.'

Gebre followed me inside and took my hand to lead me out.

'You're staying with Basha Felika now. They've given him a bigger tent. You'll be sharing it with him.'

'No!' I shouted, suddenly furious. 'I won't leave this tent. It's *my* tent now! Mr Rassam gave it to Amma.'

I think I minded more about the change of tents than I'd minded about anything else. I kicked out at Gebre, who was experienced at avoiding my flailing feet. He waited patiently until my pathetic storm had passed over, then he pointed round the tent at Mr Rassam's possessions: his boxes, his books and photograph albums and papers, his uniform chest, his folding chair and table. All trace of Amma had gone.

'Would you prefer to stay with Mr Rassam or Basha Felika?' he asked with simple cunning.

He knew the answer, but I wouldn't give him the satisfaction of saying it out loud.

I swallowed the loss of the last home I had shared with Amma. It joined the lump inside me and hardened there.

By the time we halted at Senafe the British forces had multiplied in number. As the army retreated it had gathered up all the soldiers who had been left along the way to ensure safe passage of supplies, work the telegraph system and protect the route from possible enemies.

Most of the priests who had respected Amma so deeply, and spent so many hours praying with her, had left by the time we reached Senafe. There was one, though, who stayed. His name was Aleka Zanab. I didn't know him well, though I had seen him often enough, coming out of the treasury in Magdala. He had been in charge of Father's books and papers.

Camp had already been made on our first evening at Senafe when I saw him talking with Mr Rassam and

Colonel Merewether. The three of them looked over to where I was sitting outside Basha Felika's tent, winding a belt backwards and forwards through my fingers. They smiled at me and nodded to each other. Aleka Zanab came over to me, walking in the stately manner of a priest, his long white robes swinging.

I expected him to hold out his hand-cross for me to kiss, and I was already standing up, ready to bow over it, when I saw that he wasn't carrying one after all.

'Well, Prince Alamayu,' he said, 'are you a good student? Do you know your letters?'

I stared at him, surprised. 'I . . . I think so, sir. Most of them.'

'So you can read?'

'Nearly.'

'And write?'

'A bit.'

'We'll soon improve that. I'm to be your new tutor. I'm coming to England with you.'

I studied him warily. I hadn't liked my old tutor at all and I had low expectations of tutors in general. I tried to guess how old Aleka Zanab was. His head was wrapped in a big white turban, so I couldn't see if his hair had turned grey. He looked kinder than my old teacher. He didn't carry a switch to beat me with – at least, I couldn't see one.

'That's good, sir,' I said cautiously.

'Do you say your prayers, Prince Alamayu?'

'Yes, sir.'

'Do you know the names of the saints?'

'I – I think so, sir. Amma used to . . .'

I think my voice might have wobbled a bit. In any case, he smiled and his face softened. I felt a little better. Perhaps he might turn out to be kind after all. Perhaps he wouldn't use the whip as my old teacher had done.

He said, 'Good, good. We'll start work when we reach the coast. There'll be plenty of time on the ship. We'll have a lot to do. You will be living with *ferenjis* now, Alamayu. We must make sure you don't forget your own language.'

But I have forgotten my own language, Aleka Zanab. I've forgotten almost every word of it. How can I remember it when no one has spoken it with me for so many years?

At the beginning I was nervous with Aleka Zanab and kept out of his way as much as I could. He was a famous man, a famous scholar, in Abyssinia.

It was easy to avoid him at first. I was able to stay with Basha Felika nearly all the time. If I lost sight of him for a moment, in the crowded military camp, I would freeze in panic and call for Gebre. Basha Felika was never far away and he would stride towards me on his long legs, take my hand and lead me to see whatever he was doing.

General Napier had ordered his whole army to parade in their uniforms at Senafe.

The ranks of scarlet-jacketed foot soldiers shuffled into their rows, followed by the pale blue and silver-laced splendour of the lancers. The turbaned Indians stood as straight as poles by their field guns. The mahouts waited by the heads of the elephants.

General Napier signalled to the Naval Brigade to fire their rockets. Orders rapped out through the still air. The Naval Brigade leaped into a frenzy of action. Within less than a minute the rocket tubes had been assembled, the ammunition was loaded, the officer raised his hand, the men knelt to light the fuses and the terrifying roar I hated so much was echoing back across the valley below as the missiles shot towards the high cliffs on the far side. Birds squawked in panic, and some of the mules laid their ears back and bucked, but by now a military band had started to play and the troops were marching past General Napier.

I've seen countless British military parades since then. I can sing along to the march tunes with the trombones and the clarinets. I can interpret the hoarse cries of the drill sergeants, but that first one, there at Senafe, under our Abyssinian sun, made my heart pound with feelings I couldn't have expressed: excitement perhaps, awe, and a kind of dreadful sorrow.

It didn't occur to me that I was watching my father's enemies enjoy their triumph over him. In my innocence

I could only stand there, dazzled by the uniforms and the smart marching, beating time to the music with my hand, and crowing with joy when, at a signal from a mahout, all the elephants lifted their trunks in salute.

When I grow up, I told myself, I'm going to be a soldier.

The walls are bulging again, scaring me. My head hurts and my throat is dry, and when they come, the coughing fits tear me apart. A face grows out of the wall, and it frightens me. It's my face. I can see my whole self now. I'm sitting on the dais outside Father's house, as I did in front of the chiefs. My hand rests on Gobezu's rough mane. Something metal presses down on my head. It's very heavy.

Father's words go round and round in my head.

'You are my heir,' he told me. 'You have the right to my throne.'

Another man sits on the throne of Abyssinia now, and it was the British who helped him take it. The man calls himself 'Yohannes'. King John. By what right does he sit there? Shouldn't that throne be mine?

Has God let all these things happen to me for a purpose? Would the Abyssinian child prince and the Rugby schoolboy be a good combination in the making of a king?

If ever I do become a king, what then? What kind of ruler would I be?

I could never be like Father. No one could match up to him. I'll never be as strong as he was, or as ruthless. I can't ride wild horses and inspire a whole army of men. I would never have the courage to run out alone to face an attacking army, as he did, and make them turn and flee from him in terror.

No, I'd be a different kind of king. I'd be good at studying people and listening to them. I'd know how to find out which were my enemies and which were my friends. I wouldn't give away my inner feelings. I'd be polite to everyone and make people like and trust me.

It could happen. Why not? After all, I have one great advantage that no other Abyssinian prince has ever had. I understand the *ferenjis*. I know how much they love power and want to control the rest of the world. I know their strengths, and I understand too how their ignorance makes them weak. I would know how to talk to them and make them listen to me.

Queen Victoria likes me. I would always have her on my side. She has sent me a photograph of herself. There's a message written on it in her own handwriting:

To Alamayu, from your affectionate friend, Victoria

The boys here gasped when they saw it. Everyone has shown me more respect since they heard of her photograph. A few people called me 'darkie' to my face when I first came, but they didn't dare do so again once they'd seen the Queen's photograph. I have nothing more to fear from the school bullies.

What would I have to do in order to return to Abyssinia? Relearn Amharic, of course. It shouldn't be too difficult. The language must still be locked up somewhere in my brain. I would only need a key to release it.

If only there was someone here who could teach it to me again, I would study with my whole heart. My mind would never wander as it does with all this useless Latin they make me study.

Slowly, as the British took me down from the mountains of Abyssinia to their ships anchored by the sea coast below, I left my own world behind and entered theirs. Everything was strange to me. Everything seemed like wizardry. The British had been able to take to Magdala only as much as men, mules and elephants could carry. Afterwards, I learned that they'd carried only a small number of the deadly weapons they possess, but even the ones they had astonished me. Father's armies travelled lightly, every man carrying his own shield, spear and musket. Europeans take mountains of baggage with them wherever they go. (I suppose I'm just the same now. At the end of every term, my trunk is so full of the clothes I take on holiday with me that I can barely lift it myself.)

I wasn't much impressed by the telegraph, if I am truthful. When you're seven everything seems magical, and I took it for granted. It didn't astonish me that the wires which the British had strung alongside the track could carry messages faster than a bird could fly.

I noticed the hand of God, I think, more than the works of men. The heat as we came down to those stifling deserts made me gasp and cry for water. The sand and stones underfoot were so hot that they blistered my feet. At night, in Basha Felika's tent, I tossed and turned, unable to sleep.

The desert itself was a surprise to me. I had had no idea that there were places without mountains in the world, or that the light could ever be so bright, dazzling enough to hurt my eyes. I was used by now to seeing elephants. I laughed aloud at my first sight of a camel.

I could easily ignore the men bending to look into mysterious boxes, cloths draped over their heads (I know now that they were photographers). I didn't even notice the machines the British had installed to turn sea water into drinking water.

The greatest marvel came after a bad day of travelling. The path we were following led through a deep and narrow ravine. I was hot and tired, cross with everyone that day, but Gebre and Basha Felika kept hurrying me on, whacking my mule on the rump to make him go faster.

'I don't *want* to hurry!' I kept saying. 'I want to stop! Why can't we stop here? It's shady.'

No one took any notice. Everyone was rushing. They kept looking anxiously up at the sky, and then over their shoulders.

'No stopping here,' panted Gebre. 'Come on, Prince. Kick him! Keep to a trot!'

'I won't!' I yelled at last, pulling on the reins to bring my mule to a halt. 'You can't make me!'

Gigantic hands plucked me from the mule's saddle and I was suddenly sitting in front of Basha Felika, astride his horse.

'Run on, Gebre,' he shouted. 'I've got Alamayu!'

I think I struggled and cried, but it was no good. Basha Felika simply tightened his arms around me.

'Stop that,' he said. I hadn't heard such a stern note in his voice before. 'We're in great danger here. It's been raining in the highlands. There could be a flood rushing down here at any moment.'

'There won't be! I don't believe you! There isn't even a river!'

But I was used to obeying the voice of authority, and I didn't struggle any more. I let myself be jolted along as Basha Felika spurred his horse to a canter.

He was right. That afternoon, just after the last man had emerged from between the walls of rock on to the open plain, a wall of water roared down that narrow ravine, and if anyone had remained within it they would have been swept to their death.

The camp had swollen to a vast size. It stretched across acres of ground, with long straight lines of white tents and thousands of milling animals.

When the sun had nearly gone down, a soft breeze coming off the sea made the heat a little more bearable. It was still just light enough to see by as I ran beside Basha Felika, on our way to call on Mr Rassam. Alongside us stretched long metal rails laid in twin lines across the ground. Suddenly they began to hum and shake.

'Take care, Basha Felika! An earthquake is coming!' I called out, tugging at his hand.

But he only smiled and pointed into the distance.

I think I screamed. I know I wanted to. A huge black

monster was roaring towards us, smoke and sparks shooting out of its head.

Basha Felika squatted down beside me.

'Don't be afraid, Alamayu. It's a train. You're going to ride in it tomorrow.'

I was too frightened to speak and only shook my head. The beast came closer and closer. I could see its vast wheels churning along the rails. I wanted more than anything to turn and run away, but I knew I had to show courage. I took a deep breath, screwed my eyes tight shut and waited to die.

I didn't, needless to say. I felt gusts of hot air on my face as the engine puffed past me, and I smelled for the first time the bitter smoke of coal. When I opened my eyes again a row of trucks was rattling along, and standing up in them – a sight I could hardly believe – were men, and even a pair of horses.

We did go in the train the next day. Now that I've been in so many trains, small ones and large ones, grand ones and simple ones, I know that that little train, built by the British to carry their army, with a track that they rolled up behind them like a rug and took away when they left, was as small and simple as a train could be, but I can still remember my fear and wonder when I was hoisted up to stand in one of those open trucks.

There were some other Abyssinians with us in the same truck. They treated me correctly and called me by my title. They crowded back to let Gebre lift me up so that I could see over the side. Some of their friends were running alongside the track, trying to keep up with the train. They couldn't, of course.

'We're beating them!' I shouted. 'Look! We're going faster!'

Everyone laughed.

I wish I knew where those fellows were now.

It was so hot in Zulla that I could hardly breathe, but everyone else was running about busily. Military equipment

The British camp at the port of Zulla

cluttered up the ground: towering piles of boxes, sacks, strange pieces of machinery, bundles of animal fodder, ropes, lengths of wood and cases of ammunition. Everything was laid out in neat lines and squares, in the British Army way.

The sea, although it was so close, was hardly visible. So much dust had been kicked up into the air that the water was the same colour as the sky – a kind of dull grey-brown – and the dozens of ships anchored away from the shore seemed to hang in the air, floating like gigantic birds.

People were too busy to take much notice of me. Men were rushing about, even in the terrible heat, carrying things out along the jetty. The Indians wore nothing but loincloths and turbans, while the

Englishmen sweated in their hot, heavy clothes.

I was starting to feel very strange inside. It was as if I was one of those unearthly ships, hanging between the sea and the sky, with nothing left to hold on to. People called out to me kindly. They all knew who I was. I'd learned quite a few words of English by now, from Mr Rassam and Basha Felika, but the soldiers and sailors spoke differently, and I couldn't understand them at all. Even when Basha Felika or Mr Rassam, or Gebre or Aleka Zanab, spoke to me in Amharic, I couldn't take in what they said. They might have been talking in Latin or Hindustani for all I could understand. My mind seemed to have shut down.

Basha Felika was too busy to be bothered much with me as the army prepared to embark, and I passed the next few days with my tutor. Aleka Zanab spent a lot of time sighing and worrying about whether his food had been correctly prepared. He prayed a great deal too, and I knew I mustn't interrupt him. He didn't like me going out into the camp to watch what was going on. He didn't like it either when Basha Felika came to fetch me at mealtimes to eat with some of the senior officers.

'It's Wednesday today,' he would grumble. 'It's a fasting day. The prince mustn't touch meat, or milk, or any animal produce.'

I don't think Basha Felika really understood those things. I sometimes wonder if he knew as much about Abyssinia or our Coptic religion as he thought he did. Anyway, he just smiled in his cheerful way and said, 'Don't worry, sir. I'll look after the little chap. He'll be all right and tight with me.' (Of course, he was speaking Amharic, but that's how he would have spoken if he had said it in English.)

It was all very well for Basha Felika, but I was very worried about eating forbidden things. Amma had been extremely particular and had taught me to be careful too. I'd forgotten one day that it was a Friday, when, as on a Wednesday, I was supposed to eat only vegetables and nothing that came from an animal. I had put my finger in a honey pot and licked it before I'd remembered. I'd spat the honey out at once and had run to wash out my mouth.

But in the officers' mess nobody understood or cared about forbidden food. The chief, General Napier, sat at the head of the table, which was always fancily set up with silver and china and white linen, even though it was in the middle of a desert camp, with Indian servants padding around to serve the men, but they put into their mouths things that would have made Amma gasp in horror.

The worst thing was the meat. I could never tell which animal it had come from. I didn't even realize that the long thin strip someone gave me at breakfast was bacon, from a pig. I ate it without knowing and felt very guilty afterwards. I didn't dare confess what I'd done to Aleka Zanab.

That first breakfast was the worst. I didn't know what the strange things on the table were, or how I was supposed to eat them. Someone put a piece of bread on the plate in front of me. It looked harmless enough. I waited until I thought no one was looking, then tore a piece from the edge, as I would have done if it had been *injera*, our own special bread. It tasted dry and hard, and crumbs tickled the back of my throat.

Someone noticed and clicked his fingers to one of the servants, who leaned over me and put a jar with a spoon in it by my plate. What was I supposed to do? I'd never heard of marmalade, and I hadn't been used to eating with a spoon. I stirred the spoon round in the jar for a moment or two. The stuff inside was orange and sticky. I pulled the spoon out and put it into my mouth. It was nice. I was about to take another spoonful when the servant snatched the jar away and frowned, leaving me with the spoon in my hand.

I dropped it, and froze. I thought I'd made a terrible mistake. I wanted to get down and crawl under the table, where the white cloth hanging down on all sides would have hidden me. I could see the servants exchanging scornful smiles.

'This is a bad breakfast,' I said loudly to Basha Felika. 'I want proper food. I want *injera*.'

He had been talking to General Napier and hadn't seen what was happening. Now he looked round and smiled at me.

'They don't know how to make *injera* here, Alamayu. We'll get the cook wallahs to brew you up a nice curry this evening. You'll like that.'

I think he must have seen the tears brightening my eyes, and the marmalade spoon in my hand, and the servant reproachfully holding the jar above my head.

He leaned back and took the marmalade into his own large hands, then prised the spoon from my stiff fingers.

'You do it like this, old chap. See? You spread it out on the bread. That's the dandy.'

Then General Napier said something to him in English which took everyone's attention away from me, and all the officers began to discuss something with great energy, moving knives and forks around on the white cloth as if they were demonstrating the movement of troops in some old battle. But I sat there, the bread and marmalade untouched on my plate, feeling wretched and humiliated.

It was sheer hunger in the end that drove me to eat *ferenji* food, but when I first gave in I couldn't swallow a mouthful without anxiety and shame, never knowing if I was breaking a rule of my religion. Now I don't even know what those rules were.

Aleka Zanab started giving me lessons during the few days we stayed in the camp in Zulla, before the ship we were to go on was ready to take us. He had no chalk and no slate to write on, and he would sit on a stool and scratch letters and words in the dust, making me say them out loud. I got most of them right, but I couldn't concentrate and made a lot of mistakes. It irritated him whenever I got a word wrong. His stick would hover over my head, and I would cower away from it, afraid he would hit me.

He never did. I suppose, now that I think of it, that it wasn't only my ignorance that annoyed him. The heat must have made him miserable. He wouldn't take off his thick turban or his heavy priestly robes. I think too that he was worried about the journey to come. He had never been to sea. He was ready to take me on as a solemn duty to Amma and our country, but I think he saw me as a burden and guessed I would never be a great scholar like he was.

General Napier decided that I shouldn't stay with Basha Felika any longer, but should move into Aleka Zanab's tent and sleep on a cowskin mat alongside him. I didn't want to. Aleka Zanab snored and muttered in his sleep like a tired old man. He seemed almost shy of me, and didn't know how to talk to me. I didn't dare creep near to him for comfort. If he saw that I couldn't sleep, he would only tell me to pray. I don't think he was used to children. Worst of all, I missed the reassuring presence of Basha Felika's great strength and clumsy affection.

At least Gebre came with me. He slept stretched out across the doorway of the tent, guarding me as he always had done at home.

No one told me what was happening on the day we went aboard the *Feroze*, the ship that would take us up the Red Sea to Suez. Gebre was busy from early morning packing up both my and Aleka Zanab's things. Not that I possessed very much. Amma's big Bible had been given to Basha Felika to look after for me, and I had a few clothes and my princely necklace, but everything else — Amma's embroidered dresses and *shammas*, her rugs and cushions, her jewellery and her papers — had gone. I don't know who took them. I didn't think about any of that. I was only concerned about two strange shells that I'd found lying on the sand by the edge of the water. I'd never seen anything like them before and I liked to run my fingers round their hard outer rims and touch their smooth insides. I had become attached to them and I felt a desperate anxiety if one of them was missing. They were mine. They were the only things I had left to me that were truly mine.

Aleka Zanab had been groaning and muttering in an agitated state since before dawn. I'd woken late that morning to find him rocking backwards and forwards. He was chanting prayers quietly to himself and kept breaking off to shake his head and heave great sighs. I ran out of our tent as soon as I could to find Basha Felika (I think I really wanted to eat some marmalade), but everything had changed. All the tents, including the mess tent where I had eaten with the senior officers, had disappeared. I looked around for someone, to tell them that I was hungry, but

I didn't know any of the Indian men who were hurrying everywhere, bowed down under huge loads.

I turned to go back to our own tent, but it too had disappeared. In the few minutes since I had left, Gebre had pulled it down, and I couldn't see over the tops of the piles of bales and bundles to make out where he was. I panicked and started running, crying loudly, frantic to find someone I knew. Then unknown arms snatched me up, and I was clasped to a strange, khaki-covered chest. I struggled and began to scream, but a few moments later the soldier set me down beside the heap of bags and bundles on which Aleka Zanab was sitting, with Gebre beside him, tightening a cord round the last of them.

'You're leaving today, Prince. Now. You've been called to your ship,' Gebre said gruffly, not looking at me.

'What ship? Where are we going?'

'You're going to England. You know you are. You have to start your journey today.'

A horrible fear gripped me.

'But you're coming too, Gebre, aren't you? You've *got* to come. You're my servant. You've got to do what I say.'

Aleka Zanab coughed. I don't think he knew what to do. As I said, he didn't understand children. He laid a firm hand on my shoulder and said, 'Come, Prince Alamayu. What would Gebre do over there in England? They'll give you an English servant. You won't need him any more.'

I flopped down on to the sand. I had lost my father,

my mother, my home and my old nurse, but this last loss felt like the cruellest of all. There would be no one, not one person, left to me now who knew me. No one who belonged to me. No one who was mine.

'No!' I shouted. 'You have to come! Basha Felika will let you. I'll tell General Napier that I won't go without you!'

Aleka Zanab stood up and shook out his robe. He looked down at me from what seemed like a great height.

'Stand up, Prince. Aren't you ashamed to cry over a slave? Remember who you are.'

It was what Father would have said. I knew that. Shakily I got to my feet. Gebre was wringing his hands. He knelt down beside me, as Abebech had done, so that his face was level with mine.

'Look,' he said, 'I've got your shells. I kept them out for you,' and he put them into my hands.

A shadow fell across us. I looked up to see Basha Felika standing there.

'All ready?' he said breezily. 'They're coming to fetch your things. Time to go on board. Have you said goodbye to Gebre, Alamayu? Good. Good.'

Gebre had risen to his feet. Basha Felika clapped him on the shoulder.

'You're a free man now. Where will you go?'

A half-smile crossed Gebre's face. I watched it with indignation. Surely he wasn't *glad* to leave me?

'Home,' he said. 'To my village. It's been a long time.'

Basha Felika pulled a heavy purse from his pocket and dropped it into Gebre's outstretched hand.

'This should help you in your new life,' he said. Then he put out his hand towards me, expecting me to take it and run off alongside him.

I couldn't move.

'Gebre, don't you *want* to stay with me?' I said, and I think my voice must have sounded rather small.

He bent down again.

'Of course I do, little Prince, but they won't let me. And . . . and I want to go home.'

'I want to go home too!'

It came out as a wail and I was afraid I would start to sob and make them angry. I sensed the three men above me looking at each other. Then Gebre picked me up and hugged me tightly.

'I'll never forget you. You'll come back soon to Abyssinia. I'll be waiting for you.'

A long blast on a whistle came from the end of the jetty. Basha Felika held out his arms and Gebre passed me into them, but I broke free and dropped to the ground.

I pulled myself up to my full height, remembering some words that I'd heard Father say.

'God go with you, Gebre. I dismiss you from my service.'

Then, still clutching my shells, I walked away from him, between Basha Felika and Aleka Zanab, refusing to hold either of their hands. I don't think I looked back. I can't remember now. All I do know is that when I stepped on to the ship I felt something strange because a wave had hit the high white bows and the ship was rocking. I thought the whole world was heaving under my feet.

Everything frightened me on the SS *Feroze*. I think it was the depth of the water beneath its metal hull that scared me first, and the way the ship never kept still, shifting about on the waves, so that I had to clutch at something just to stay on my feet. Holding on to rails was unpleasant after mid-morning, because by then the heat was so intense that anything made of metal was scorching to touch.

They gave Aleka Zanab and me a small cabin next to General Napier's. It was so stiflingly hot that I couldn't bear to stay in it for more than a few minutes at a time. I tore off my tunic (I was still wearing Abyssinian clothes) and opened one of the bundles that Gebre had packed to look for something cooler to wear. I couldn't find anything, and left my things strewn across the floor of the cabin. I was used to a servant looking after me. I didn't know about tidying things away.

We hadn't been on board for more than a short while when the ship's engines started up with a terrible clanking and grinding sound. I think it frightened Aleka Zanab nearly as much as me. He was clutching the stem of his brass hand-cross, and I saw his knuckles go pale. He tried to comfort me, I do remember that, but he didn't know how to go about it as Gebre would have done.

'There's no need to fear,' he said, nervously licking his lips. 'Our Lord is the master of the seas. Even the winds and the waves obey Him. Stop staring out of that porthole, Prince. There's nothing to see out there except for the land of the Muslim infidel. Come and sit on the bunk beside me. We'll read from the Bible together.'

I couldn't bear the heat a moment longer.

'I need to go up on deck,' I said, as respectfully as I could. 'I have to find Basha Felika.'

I slipped out through the door and up the stairway to the deck, where the air was hardly fresh but at least there was more of it.

The ship was already a good distance from the shore and the coastline of Africa was steadily slipping past. I watched the sailors in their white uniforms. They were setting up awnings on the deck so that General Napier and his staff could sit in the shade and enjoy the breeze from the sea.

Suddenly I thought of my shells and I was dreadfully afraid in case they were lost. The idea that I might lose them filled me with panic. They were the only things that I now possessed, the only things that connected me with home. My heart beat fast as I rushed back down to our cabin. Another Abyssinian man was there. He was kneeling on the floor, his back towards me, massaging Aleka Zanab's feet. I caught the whiff of a strange smell and I thought it must be coming from him. I stared at him disapprovingly.

'Who are you? What are you doing in here?' I said.

He stood up, and bowed to me in the correct way, so I nodded at him, trying to hold my head up high, like Father always told me to.

'I'm Kassa, Your Highness,' he said. 'Basha Felika has hired me. I'm your new servant.'

I was used to Gebre's squeaky voice, which all our eunuchs had, but this Kassa had the deep voice of a man.

'Where are my shells?' I demanded. 'Give them to me at once.'

'Shells?' He looked puzzled.

'Don't run away again, Prince,' Aleka Zanab said severely. 'We have our work to do.'

'I can't stop, sir. I'm sorry, but I've got to find my shells.' I sounded as respectful as I could.

He started saying something, but then stopped and held a corner of his *shamma* to his nose. His face had turned a strange grey colour. The ship tilted sideways, and he bent over, holding on to his stomach and groaning.

I fled, thinking perhaps that I'd left my shells on the deck. I met Basha Felika as I came out at the top of the stairway.

'There you are, old fellow. Come on. Let me show

you the ship. You'll like her.'

The desperate need to find my shells receded.

I'll look for them later, I thought. They'll be in the cabin somewhere.

It was impossible not to feel safe when you were with Basha Felika. He was so big, so strong and so confident that he seemed like a fortress of a man. He towered over everyone, and his arms were like strong walls.

The *Feroze* was really was quite a small ship (though it didn't seem small to me then). The only passengers were General Napier, some senior officers with their servants, some men who kept writing and drawing all the time, Basha Felika, Aleka Zanab, me and our man Kassa.

I was Basha Felika's devoted follower for the rest of the evening, and when night fell I stayed on deck with him as long as I could. I couldn't bear the idea of going below into the heat of our cabin to face the disapproving looks of Aleka Zanab. Basha Felika settled himself on a coil of rope beside the rail, and I leaned against him. We looked out across the water, on which the moon had made a silvery path. There were animals playing in the sea. They would shoot up into the air, shaking silvery drops around them, then dive down again and disappear.

'Porpoises,' Basha Felika said.

'Porp-orp . . .' I tried to say, but I was so sleepy that the end of the word was lost in a yawn.

'Time you were in bed, old chap,' said Basha Felika, prodding me towards the stairway.

The bad smell in our cabin was much worse. I'd been sleepy, but it woke me up. Aleka Zanab was already lying on his bunk facing the wall, with Kassa lying on the floor beside him. I decided to tell Kassa that he'd have to sleep outside and take his smell with him, but there was something that I wanted him to do first.

'Wake up, Kassa,' I said, nudging him with my foot. 'I want my shells. Where are they?'

He sat up, rubbing his head. He was still half asleep.

'Your . . . ?' he said stupidly.

A grunt came from Aleka Zanab's bunk. He was awake after all.

'Forget about those silly shells, prince. Settle down. It's time to sleep.'

I tried to obey him. I lay down and closed my eyes, but the heat and the stench were too much, even for him. We tossed and turned for a while, then he heaved a sigh and said, 'Roll up your mat, Alamayu. There's no help for it. We'll have to go up and sleep on deck.'

I knew he didn't like the idea. He disliked the night air. It wasn't really safe, he said, to sleep in the open. Decent people only did so when they had no alternative. Evil forces were at work. We would have to say special prayers in order to keep wickedness away.

He was surprised to find that the deck was crowded. Everyone else seemed to have had the same idea. Nearly all the passengers were lying out under the stars. Most of the officers were not yet asleep, and I could see the tips of their cheroots glowing in the darkness as they smoked and talked in quiet voices over the low hum of the ship's engines. Basha Felika wasn't among them. He seemed to be the only one who could bear the heat below and was sleeping in his cabin.

Aleka Zanab chose a place apart from the others, near the base of the funnel, and we spread out our mats. But I had only one idea in my head.

'I want my shells!' I said.

Aleka Zanab didn't take any notice.

'I can't go to sleep without my shells!' I insisted, my voice rising. 'Kassa, go and find them.'

Aleka Zanab sighed with exasperation. 'I told you to forget about them,' he said. 'What did you want them for anyway? They've gone. I threw them out of the porthole. They had creatures inside them that had died. Couldn't you smell them? Even after I'd thrown them away it was quite overpowering.'

I stood staring at him, perfectly still. Everything that had happened to me, all the horrible things, seemed to rise up inside me at that moment, and I was consumed with a rage so terrible that if I'd had the strength I would have struck my old tutor to the ground. Instead, I threw myself down on to the deck and drummed my heels on the boards. It makes me feel hot with shame to think of it now.

I was so blinded by fury that I was unaware of anyone else, but after a while I sensed another presence and saw a pair of legs planted on the deck beside me. A stern voice spoke in English. It had such authority that I stopped in mid-scream and looked up to see the commander-in-chief, General Napier himself, staring down at me. I picked myself up off the deck and hurled myself at him, shouting out that Aleka Zanab was a thief and an evil man, and that he should be thrown into the sea.

General Napier couldn't understand me of course. He stood perplexed for a moment, then picked me up and strode down the stairway to the passage leading to the cabins below, holding me under his arm with my legs kicking out

General Napier

behind as if I was a dog. The next thing I knew, we were in Basha Felika's cabin and I had been handed over to him.

Basha Felika was in his bunk. He sat up, his red hair and beard rumpled. He said something in English, his voice thick with sleep.

The extreme anger I had felt had now turned into a dreadful anguish, and I was eaten up with fear, a terror so great that I could do nothing but throw myself against Basha Felika's chest and sob.

He stood up, almost cracking his head against the low ceiling of the cabin. Then with me in his arms he sank back down on to his bunk, saying gently, 'It's all right, young man. I'm here now. There's nothing to be afraid of. What happened to you? Why are you so upset?'

I didn't know. For some reason I could tell no one about the loss of my shells. The image of them falling, falling, out of the porthole and sinking down into the water was too horrible to me. I felt as if I was falling too, and that I was going to drown. Once such a thought had entered my mind, other even more horrifying images crowded in. I saw Father lying dead in that dismal hut, and Amma being pushed into that cold stone tomb, and the King's House at Magdala in flames. And all the time my shells were sinking away out of reach, flung into the sea by Aleka Zanab.

'Aleka Zanab, he's a bad man,' I managed to say, hiccuping between my sobs. 'He wants to hurt me.'

'No, no,' said Basha Felika soothingly. 'That's foolish, Alamayu. He's your tutor. A learned man, a good man.'

I shook my head so hard that my neck hurt.

'He isn't. He . . . He has the evil eye!'

I knew that that was the worst thing you could say about anyone. Abebech had warned me many times about people who had the evil eye. Amma had told me horrible stories too. If someone with the evil eye looked at you, you could fall sick or go mad. You could even die. All kinds of terrible things could happen to you.

As soon as I'd said those fatal words I began to believe them. There was something odd, I now thought, in the way that Aleka Zanab looked at me. His eyes weren't entirely straight. One seemed to look a bit to the side. Perhaps he was an evil spirit who had caused all the dreadful things that had happened.

'I don't want to see him ever again!' I cried, beginning to sob again, and hanging on to Basha Felika with all my strength, as if I was sure that someone would try to tear me away from him. 'Don't take me back to him! I won't go!'

It was a long time before my storm of crying died down, and Basha Felika had only to loosen his arms for a moment for me to break out into even more desperate wails. At last he said, 'Look here, old chap, there's no need to get into such a state. I won't take you back to your cabin. How would you like to stay with me tonight? We'll ask the chief if he'll let you. It'll all look much better in the morning.'

I saw then that General Napier was still there, standing by the cabin door. The two men spoke briefly in English, then Basha Felika said, 'That's all right then. No need for any more tears. You'll stay here with me, and you'll be quite safe. I'm so big and clumsy that evil eyes don't work on me. They just bounce off. Always have.'

That little cabin was hot, all right, but Basha Felika had

opened his porthole and a little freshness came in off the sea. It wasn't suffocating like the one I had shared with Aleka Zanab. Terror still held me in its grip. I couldn't bear to let go of Basha Felika, and when he made up a little bed for me on the floor I shook my head and refused to lie on it. I was keeping my eyes on the door, convinced that it would fly open and that Aleka Zanab, who in my imagination was now a terrifying monster, would be standing there, claw-like hands held out to grab me and fling me into the sea to my death. So when Basha Felika lay down on his bunk and gave a mighty yawn I crept across to him and climbed in beside him. He had left the lamp burning low, and I saw him open one sleepy eye.

'Too scared to sleep alone?' he said. 'Oh, very well. Just for tonight. But try not to wriggle, eh?'

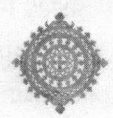

The terror that struck me that night on the *Feroze*, with the Red Sea slapping against her hull and the cold moon making ghostly shadows on her deck, was the most intense I've ever felt. Thinking about it even now makes my breath come faster. It took a long time to die down. Echoes of it came back to me for years afterwards. I would be struck with it out of the blue and stop dead whatever I was doing, standing rigid in a paralysing panic.

I don't like the thought of myself as I was then, a silly child, screaming like a hysterical girl because I'd lost a couple of shells. I don't much like the thought of myself when I first came to Rugby, and how I used to dodge round corners to hide from bullies.

To be a king you need to be more than a strong man who can leap from the ground on to a horse. You need first to be master of yourself and your fears. You need to know who your enemies are, and which of your friends you can trust.

I'm sorry now that it ended so badly with Aleka Zanab. I wish I'd been given the time to get to know him better and get over my anguish over losing those shells. I realized this last term when someone brought a bag of cockles and winkles into Elsee's, and we had a shellfish feast in Bull's study. You have to dig the meat out of a winkle. The creature hides right up inside the curls of its shell. One of them had gone bad and the smell was so nasty that Bull rushed to open his window and throw the thing out.

The stench brought the memory of that night on the *Feroze* roaring back to me again. I could see Aleka Zanab lying there on the deck, his white robes gleaming in the moonlight, his old eyes blinking up at me in puzzlement, and the officers I had woken with my screams propping themselves up on their elbows to see what was happening, and the long legs of the chief standing beside me, and the black bulk of the ship's funnel rearing up behind him.

At that moment, when Bull threw the bad winkle out of his study window, I understood what I had done and the mistake I had made. In turning against my tutor I had turned against my country.

If Aleka Zanab had stayed with me, if he'd kept my language alive in me, taught me our history and our stories, kept me faithful to our special prayers, our saints and our traditions, it would have been easier for me to go home and work to take back my throne. It will be much, much harder for me now.

I don't think that General Napier should have listened to my childish fears. He shouldn't have dismissed Aleka Zanab so quickly, but that's what he did. As soon as we reached the port of Suez he paid him off and sent him home to Abyssinia. I stupidly believed I had scored a triumph. I thought that I would never have to sit through boring lessons again and be scolded for not paying attention. If only I had had more sense! Now I have to sit, hour after hour, puzzling over stupid Latin, which is of no use to me at all. If Aleka Zanab came back to me, here at Rugby, and spoke to me in Amharic, if he talked to me about the great kings and chiefs who were my ancestors, I would listen eagerly to every word.

It was easier for the British, I suppose, to send the old man away. There would be no need to pay for his food or his lodgings. They wouldn't have to worry about finding someone to translate for him. Perhaps they never wanted me to return to Abyssinia and claim my father's crown. We'll see. They might get a surprise, one of these days.

It took a week for the *Feroze* to chug up the Red Sea to Suez. All that time I refused absolutely to speak to the old tutor or even to go near him. Kassa tried to coax me, but I became so upset whenever Aleka Zanab's name was mentioned that Basha Felika told him not to bother any more.

The ground felt funny underfoot when I stepped off the ship at Suez, tightly clutching Basha Felika's hand.

'Be careful, Basha Felika! There's another earthquake!' I cried out.

He laughed.

'No earthquake, old chap. You've got your sea legs on, that's all. You have to get them used to being on land again.'

Basha Felika always stands out in a crowd. He's taller than anyone else, and his flaming hair glows like fire. I thought at first that the little crowd following us as we walked away from the quayside and into the crowded city were curious about him but then I heard a voice in Amharic call out, '*Ye Tewodros lij!*' ('It's Theodore's son!') and I realized that there were people in Suez who knew about me.

I had been eagerly looking about, holding tight to Basha Felika's hand for safety, excited to be in a new place where there was so much of interest to see, but when I heard that I dropped Basha Felika's hand and forced myself to slow down, hold my head up straight and look serious. Basha Felika noticed that I was lagging behind him. He turned and told me to hurry up. I frowned at him. Even

people who couldn't speak English could tell that his voice
lacked respect. Then I saw a pucker of anxiety between his
eyebrows.

'Not sure how friendly they are here,' he explained.
'Some of your father's enemies probably came to Suez to
escape from him. We'd better not stay around too long.'

My heart jumped with fright and I quickened my step,
still trying to look dignified.

Basha Felika let out his breath with relief as we emerged
on to a broader street.

'It's all right now. Look, some of our men are over
there. British sailors. No one will try anything on with
them around.'

The British. My destroyers. My protectors. My enemies.
My friends.

Basha Felika was in search of some new clothes. His jackets
and trousers, like all those belonging to the British troops,
were stained and shabby and full of rips after travelling
along rough trails in Abyssinia and living in tents for
months at a time.

The Suez merchants saw him coming from a long way
off. They called out to him one after the other as we passed
their shops.

'This way, sir. Come here, sir! Very nice new trousers. Special price!'

Basha Felika waved at them but marched on until we came to a dark stairway between two shopfronts.

'Up you go,' he said, pushing me in front of him.

An old man sat cross-legged beside the open window. He had been sewing, but he put his needle down at the sight of us. He scrambled to his feet and came towards us, his hands outstretched.

'Captain Speedy! You are back in Suez. Safe and well, I see, thanks be to God.' His eyes travelled down Basha Felika's long length and I could see that the state of his customer's clothes pained him.

Basha Felika smiled. 'The price of soldiering. It's been hot work in Abyssinia.'

At least, I suppose that that's how their conversation went. It was half in English and half in Arabic, and I could understand only a few of the English words and none of the Arabic. But I didn't need words to see what was happening. The tailor clicked his fingers and a young boy appeared, who nodded and ran off down the stairs. Another young man stepped out from behind a curtain and began to measure Basha Felika from his shoulder to his waist.

'No, no time,' said Basha Felika. They spoke some more, and I recognized the word 'train'.

I lost interest. I wandered over to a rack on which some small clothes were hanging.

The boy came back up the stairs with a tray of little tea glasses. The young man was bringing out pair after pair of trousers, trying them against Basha Felika's long legs. All of them were too short. I reached up and felt the material of a little suit of clothes hanging on the rack. It was like the uniform that sailors wore, but it was made for a child and I could see that it might fit me. The trousers and jacket were white, and there was a square-cut collar with a blue stripe around it.

'Try it on, Alamayu!' called out Basha Felika, who had given up hope of finding trousers to fit him and was sitting on the rug beside the tailor, leaning against some cushions and sipping tea.

The young man helped me take off my Abyssinian tunic and drawers and held out the stiff white canvas trousers for me to step into. Then he slipped the jacket on and did up the buttons. Finally he perched a straw boater with ribbons dangling down the back on to my head. My head had last been shaved weeks ago and tight black curls now covered my scalp. They helped the boater to stay on.

The young man turned me round to look in the long mirror and I crowed with delight. 'Look at me, Basha Felika! I'm a sailor man now!'

He smiled. 'You look just like an English boy, but you still need shoes.'

He said something to the young man, who nodded and ran out of the room.

I think I felt a pang at the mention of shoes. At least, I hope I did. I don't like to remember the way I threw off my Abyssinian clothes so easily and enjoyed parading up and down in the uniform of a British sailor. The shoes would surely have made me pause. To Father they were a mark of decadence. A sign of weakness. But when the young man hurried back in, several pairs of elastic-sided boots under his arm, I couldn't resist trying them on, and when I found a pair that fitted and saw how smart I looked, I couldn't drag myself away from the mirror. It was the first time in my whole life that I had been able to look at myself from head to toe. Amma had had only small hand-mirrors, so up till then I had only ever seen my face.

I would have left my Abyssinian clothes lying in a heap on the tailor's floor, forgotten and discarded, if Basha Felika hadn't had them bundled up to carry back to the ship. I strutted beside him, as proud as a rooster, showing off to the bystanders, all fear of them forgotten.

'*Habash!*' I heard them say. 'Abyssinian! Theodore's son!'

Aleka Zanab had gone by the time we returned to the *Feroze*. I didn't even notice. By then I was more and more obsessed by my need to be with Basha Felika, and if he was out of my sight for even a moment I would be seized with panic. I had only been able to enjoy dressing up in my new clothes because he had been there, watching and encouraging me. It was only because I had been holding his hand that I had been able to walk with any confidence through the streets of Suez.

A special train had been laid on to take General Napier, the senior officers, Basha Felika and me across the dusty hot sands of Egypt to the port of Alexandria. The elephants had been despatched back to India. The finest treasures of Magdala were already on their way to the British Museum in London. The troops in their troopships were at sea, en route for India or for Portsmouth.

I suppose I was honoured by being part of General Napier's retinue, with the chief himself. I took it for granted. I would have expected nothing less. But now I think that I was for them only a trophy. A human curiosity. A souvenir.

Souvenirs lose their value as time passes. They're put to the back of the shelf and the maids forget to dust them.

I had become Basha Felika's determined shadow. It was my loneliness and terror that made me cling to him at first. It was only later that I truly came to love him, and I still do. It makes me feel disloyal even to think this, but I know that in some ways Basha Felika was more truly like my father than the Emperor Theodore ever was. What happened later wasn't his fault. He would never have willingly abandoned me.

We sailed to England in a troopship called HMS *Urgent*.

I was picking up more and more words of English by now. I could even understand some of the things that the sailors said to me, like 'Come here . . . Be careful . . . Look over there.' I would try repeating them only to Basha Felika. I was afraid that anyone else would laugh at me.

People were sorry for me, I think. Even General Napier tried to amuse me. He had a ball made, and he called me up to the deck to play with him. I'd never seen a ball before. When he threw it to me I didn't understand that I was supposed to catch it and throw it back to him. The ball rolled away across the deck and I stood still and did nothing.

He pointed to it, indicating that I should pick it up. I can remember the flash of anger I felt. I crossed my arms on my chest and frowned at the chief, while he went to pick up the ball.

Basha Felika was leaning against the foremast, puffing away at his pipe.

'Why didn't you pick it up, Alamayu?' he called out.

'I'm a king's son,' I shouted back furiously. 'Let him fetch his thing himself.'

It makes me smile at myself to think that I didn't know what a ball was for. It's the middle of the afternoon now, and I can hear shouts coming from the Close. There must be a game of football going on. Normally I'd be one of the crowd on the sidelines cheering on one team or the other, if I wasn't playing myself. I hope someone comes and tells me about it. I'll want to know who's played well, and which side has won.

The English are mad about games. At least we are at Rugby. There's cricket in the summer and Rugby football in the winter.

'The sports of a great public school are the foundation of a manly character,' booms Dr Jex-Blake, our headmaster, when he congratulates a team after a victory.

There's a lot of talk here about being 'manly'. It's manly to be brave and play a decent game and tell the truth. It's not manly to cry or bully younger boys or loll about daydreaming. Father was manly, there's no doubt about that. I'm manly on the outside – at least I try to be – but inside I don't know who or what I am. I don't feel very manly at the moment, that's certain. How can I feel manly when I can hardly lift my head off the pillow?

I learned very soon about picking up balls and throwing them back. It's a good thing I did. In this school it's just as important to get into a top team as it is to win a Latin prize. When a fellow does especially well in a match and scores a try against the odds, his teammates hoist him up on to their shoulders and carry him off the Close back into the quad, while all the others throw their caps in the air and give three cheers. It hasn't happened to me yet, but it will one day, I know, if only I can get better.

I was all right on the voyage back to England as long as I was with Basha Felika. Night times were the worst. Every time I was put to bed and tried to go to sleep I would be afraid that he would disappear and leave me completely alone. I refused to shut my eyes at all unless he held me in his arms. And if I woke up in the night I'd wriggle and cry until he woke up too, and I'd beg him to guard me until I was asleep again.

Everything in England was new to me. Everything was a shock. The oddest thing was that almost everyone was a *ferenji*. I saw a few dark-skinned men working around the ships at the dock where we landed, but they didn't look like Abyssinians. There was no one, except for Kassa, who looked at all like me.

I don't remember being surprised by the crowds that had gathered on the quayside in Plymouth, waiting to see me. People at home had always run to watch when I went past in the royal procession. It was what I expected, but Basha Felika was astonished and even alarmed.

He hesitated at the top of the gangway down which we had to walk off the ship.

'Phew!' he muttered. 'Now we're for it.'

It was usually I who held on to his hand with all my strength, but this time he was clutching mine, nearly crushing it in his great fist.

Once we were down on dry land and among the crowd I began to feel uneasy too. At home people would have bowed and the women would have made their high *la-la-la* cries. These people showed no respect. They shoved each other out of the way to get close to me and I was afraid they would come right up and pull at me. Luckily an officer still on board saw what was happening and sent some sailors running down the gangway. They surrounded us and cleared a path so that we could hurry through to the carriage that was waiting to take us to the train station.

We had our own compartment on the train that took us to Portsmouth. It was a nicer train than the Egyptian one I had been on from Suez to Alexandria. I looked out of the window at first. Everything was strange to me. Basha Felika told me that the towers sticking up out of the villages were churches. I was glad to see them, for Amma's sake, and I bowed whenever we saw one after that, as she would have done, only the train went so fast and there were so many churches that I had to give up after a while. The best thing was that I could see cows and sheep and horses in the fields. I craned my neck to spot the children who should have been looking after them, but I never saw any.

After a while I fell asleep.

I don't remember much about Portsmouth. There was a hotel, we ate our meals in a smoky dining room, serious men came to talk to Basha Felika, and a tailor brought me some new suits of clothes.

'On the move again today,' Basha Felika said to me at breakfast, a couple of days after we had arrived in Portsmouth.

I didn't answer. Everywhere seemed strange to me. I didn't mind where I went as long as I was with Basha Felika.

'They're taking us over to the island in a yacht,' he said. 'With the Chief. With General Napier himself. It's a great honour. Today's the day.'

'What island?' I said, holding a lump of sugar high above my teacup and wondering if it would make the tea splash into the saucer.

'The Isle of Wight. We're going to Osborne. To meet the Queen — Queen Victoria herself! She's granting us an audience today.'

His voice sounded funny, as if he had something stuck in his throat which needed a lot of coughing to clear. I stared at him and made a discovery. Basha Felika was scared.

'You're scared,' I said.

He took a swig of tea, then wiped his bushy moustache with an unsteady hand.

'Me? Of course I'm not scared!'

'Yes, you are,' I said.

I was pleased. It was usually I who was scared, but not this time. It was correct for ordinary people to be scared when they were about to meet a king. They were always

terrified of Father, even the great chiefs. I had often seen
how they trembled and how sweat broke out on their faces.
It was only natural for Basha Felika to be frightened, but I
was quite calm. This monarch was no greater than Father,
even though she ruled over many more lands. I didn't
know about her ancestors, but I was sure that she was not
descended from King Solomon, as I am, and anyway, she
was only a woman.

'I'll wear my velvet suit,' I said, pleased at the thought.

'I think she'd like to see you in your Abyssinian clothes,'
Basha Felika said, but he didn't sound very certain.

'I *want* my velvet suit,' I said crossly.

I was afraid that Basha Felika would insist, so I hunted
around in my head for a reason.

'Father liked it when you wore Abyssinian clothes for
him,' I said at last, nodding triumphantly. 'The Queen will
think I'm just being polite if I dress like an English boy.'

He smiled. 'You win. But wear your necklace.'

I considered this and nodded. 'I will.'

The waiter had brought him his usual breakfast – a large
plate of kidneys and fried eggs – but he pushed it away.

'Not hungry today,' he said. 'Come on, young man.
Let's get ourselves ready.'

Queen Victoria is lucky, I think. There are no chiefs trying to take her throne away from her. She doesn't have to travel around the country with an army, dealing with rebels who would kill her if they could. I don't understand why she remains so powerful. She sits there, in her big house on the Isle of Wight, a long way from her capital, hardly moving out of her chair, while ministers and generals and other kings and princes put themselves out to travel across the water to see her and kneel at her feet.

The boys here at Rugby don't have to show respect to the Queen because there are no spies here to report on them (at least, as far as I know). Yet they hold the royal family in greater regard than anyone. At a school concert, they start off by singing 'God bless the Prince of Wales', and at the end they all stand up to sing 'God Save the Queen'.

There are pictures of the Queen in some of the shops in Rugby, with flags around them. And when it's her birthday they deck the whole town in bunting and the band plays and there are processions and speeches to celebrate.

No one here quite believes that I know Queen Victoria, in spite of the signed photograph she sent me, which I keep in my study. They ask me about her all the time, but I never say very much. Princes don't gossip about each other.

Her friendship for me puzzles them. They don't say it, but I know that some of them think it's wrong that a 'darkie' – a 'savage' – a 'native' – like me is a friend and a favourite of their revered Queen. Somehow, they don't think it's fair. And she *is* my friend. She has sent me a kind letter since I've been ill, hoping that I'll get better quickly and asking me to come and see her when I'm well again. I'll show it to Dr Jex-Blake. To him, a request from the Queen should be a command.

It was by the queen's command that her own yacht came to fetch and take us over to Cowes on the Isle of Wight. It was a very smart boat. The bosun had a whistle, and whenever he blew it the sailors jumped to their work. General Napier was already standing on the deck when Basha Felika and I went on board. He greeted me in a friendly way, but I saw that there were drops of sweat on his forehead. He seemed almost as nervous of seeing the Queen as Basha Felika.

'Where's our cabin?' I asked Basha Felika as we stood on the deck.

'We don't need one. It's a very short journey. We'll be there in less than an hour.'

The coast of the island was already coming up fast in front of us.

A sailor lifted me down on to the jetty. The boatswain blew his whistle again and the yacht was ready to leave. A man with long side whiskers and a beaky nose was waiting for us. As we approached, he was looking at a large gold watch, but he slid it back into his waistcoat pocket and held out his hand to Sir Robert Napier, then to Basha Felika, and smiled at me. The men started to talk in English.

'We're to walk up to the house,' Basha Felika said to me, brushing a speck of something off the sleeve of his scarlet uniform. 'Her Majesty is expecting us.'

I could see a big house painted a funny yellow colour at the top of a small hill. The three men walked on fast, their heads together as they talked. I ran after them.

Since I had left Africa, I had only been at sea or in a city, first in Suez, then Alexandria, then Portsmouth. It felt like a long time since I had walked on a country path, among grass and trees and stones, and I had never before done it while wearing a pair of boots. My feet felt awkward. The men were going too fast for me to keep up with them. As the distance between us increased, I began to feel afraid. Overhead, little white clouds were tumbling uncomfortably fast across the sky. Close by the path was a thick clump of trees and bushes. The wind rustled through the leaves.

I started to shiver. I couldn't walk on.

'Basha Felika!' I cried out. 'Take care! There are lions in that jungle!'

Basha Felika turned and hurried back to me. He said something to General Napier, who smiled. I felt my face grow hot. I hated it when people laughed at me.

'There are no lions here,' Basha Felika said, taking my hand in his. 'No leopards, or elephants, or hyenas.'

'Well, there should be,' I said indignantly. 'Proper kings always have lions.'

'Oh, Victoria's a proper queen all right,' he said, 'lions or no lions,' and he ran a finger round the inside of his collar as if it was too tight for him.

Queen Victoria's house on the Isle of Wight is called Osborne. It seemed huge to me. It went up and up so high that I had to lean my head back to see the top of the tower

Osbourne, Queen Victoria's home on the Isle of Wight

that rose up from the middle of it. Of course, I hadn't been to London then. I know now that Osborne isn't a real palace. It's not even as big as many quite ordinary buildings in British towns.

We walked along paths between areas of grass that had been cut as smooth as velvet and came into a sort of courtyard. The house stretched round three sides of it. There seemed to be hundreds of windows. They looked like eyes to me, and I felt as if they were staring at me. I began to shrink inside and my feet slowed down until I could barely walk.

Basha Felika bent over me. 'Are you all right? Do you want me to carry you?'

I shook my head. 'No.'

He took my hand. His own was clammy with nervous sweat. His mood infected me and I began to shiver.

The great doors ahead of us had swung open. Two men stood there, one on either side. They were enormous — as tall as Basha Felika. They had shiny black shoes, white stockings, scarlet coats trimmed with gold, and stiff white hair with rows of neat curls at the side.

'Are they princes?' I whispered to Basha Felika. 'Are they Queen Victoria's sons?'

'No, they're servants. Footmen. It's their job to open the door for us.'

I was glad I had asked him. I might have made a mistake and bowed to them.

The man who had walked with us from the jetty said something to one of the footmen, who turned stiffly and began to walk down a corridor inside.

'Here we go,' said Basha Felika.

The corridor was wide. There were patterns and colours everywhere, even on the floor, which had strange pictures of fishes made of little squares of coloured stone. The footman's shoes seemed to have soft soles, but Basha Felika's uniform boots made a loud noise that echoed off the walls. He started to walk a bit funnily, almost on tiptoe, trying to be quiet. Sir Robert Napier didn't seem to mind the noise he made. He marched forward down the corridor, his dress sword swinging, as if he was about to confront an enemy.

Everything was shiny and hard and cold in that corridor, and all the way along it there were statues of people in white stone. I had never seen statues before and I jumped with fright at the sight of the first one. I thought it was the head and shoulders of a dead person, one of the Queen's enemies, perhaps, but as we came up to it I saw that it wasn't real.

The footman turned a corner and we went after him, down another corridor. Now I could hear the sound of music coming from behind a door. Someone was playing on an instrument. A dog yapped, and a girl's voice called to it to be quiet.

The footman stopped outside a door. Another footman, just as tall and dressed in the same magnificent red and gold coat, was standing to attention there. They nodded to each other, and the second one opened the door.

'Prince Alamayu of Abyssinia, ma'am,' he said loudly. 'General Sir Robert Napier, and Captain Speedy.'

I was expecting the Queen to be sitting on a beautiful rug spread over a couch with a lot of silk cushions piled up behind her, as Father used to do when he was receiving important guests. I knew there wouldn't be any lions, but I was at least expecting crowds of servants to be standing behind her throne. The room we stepped into wasn't even very big. There weren't any men in it, only three or four women. A couple of them were sitting at a table. They

seemed to have been sewing, but they put their work
down when we came into the room. There was a fair girl
with a long face and big blue eyes who looked about ten or
eleven years old. She jumped up and came across to me,
but she stopped before she reached me and looked down,
her cheeks turning pink. I thought she was shy.

The other woman in the room was quite old and fat.
She was sitting on a straight chair, and I could see that she
was very short. She was dressed all in black except for a
white cloth cap on her head.

There was no one in the room who looked like a queen.
I waited, expecting to be taken somewhere else. Then I saw
that something strange had happened to Basha Felika. His
face had gone red and he was breathing shortly. I was afraid
that he would lunge across the room and crash into one of
the many little tables, sending all the things on it flying, as
he had done when he had come into Amma's tent.

Luckily Sir Robert Napier moved first. He crossed the
floor and dropped on one knee in front of the old woman,
his head bowed.

'Your Majesty,' he said.

I knew those English words. They meant *Jan Hoy*. This
old woman was the Queen.

Sir Robert stood up and bowed again. The Queen was
looking past him now, towards Basha Felika and me. I saw
that she was smiling. She lifted her hand to call us over to her.

Basha Felika took a deep breath and surged across the

room, coming to a halt just in time in front of the Queen. He too knelt down in front of her. He had let go of my hand now. I didn't think it was right for me to kneel as well. Royal people don't kneel down to each other. I didn't feel at all afraid. This great Queen was only an old woman in a plain dress. I still couldn't quite believe that she was the famous Queen Victoria, the person who had sent her armies to Abyssinia and caused my father's death.

I went to the table and stood beside her. I wasn't quite sure what to do next.

She put out her arm and actually pulled me to her side. She was so short that her head wasn't much higher than mine. Then she said something to Basha Felika and he stood up and went to stand beside Sir Robert at the side of the room. He cleared his throat and spoke for a minute or two. She nodded, and put out her hand to finger my royal necklace. Basha Felika spoke again.

The dress that the Queen was wearing was stiff and shiny so that it shone in the light even though it was black. It rustled when she moved. Her face was quite fleshy and pale. It looked as if it had been dusted with powder. She didn't smell like a person, but like flowers. I didn't know English flowers then, but now I know that she smelled of lavender.

She bent over me and kissed my cheek. Her own was very soft. I stood absolutely still.

She released me after a moment and I stepped back,

Queen Victoria

nearly bumping into another table behind me. She called
Basha Felika to come nearer and started asking him
questions again. As he answered, her eyes were on me. She
looked kind and sympathetic, and every now and then she
sighed.

'The Queen wants to know,' Basha Felika said suddenly
in Amharic, 'if you say your prayers like your dear mama
taught you.'

'Yes,' I said, though I realized guiltily that I had forgotten some of them already.

She beckoned to the young girl who was standing behind me.

'Beatrice, dear,' she said, and nodded at a fruit bowl on yet another table.

The girl – I know now that it was Princess Beatrice, the Queen's youngest daughter – picked up a peach and put it into my hand. She didn't say anything, but she didn't look quite so shy any more.

I remembered suddenly some words that Mr Rassam had taught me, my very first in English.

'Me tank you verra much,' I said.

Everyone laughed. The two young ladies who had been sewing (they were princesses too) raised their hands to their mouths and tittered politely. The Queen laughed loudly, showing her little teeth. Even the footman standing by the door cracked a small smile. Only the youngest princess didn't laugh. She nodded at me encouragingly. She could see how uncomfortable I was.

'That went very well,' Basha Felika said with a sigh of relief as the door closed behind us. 'Her Majesty took a real fancy to you. She loves children.'

We set off behind the footman to walk back down the long corridors to the front door, leaving Sir Robert inside the room with the Queen and the princesses.

I shook my head.

'They all laughed at me,' I said.

I was squeezing the peach too tightly. I had never had one before and I didn't realize that juice would drip from it.

'They weren't laughing at you. Not really. They were showing you how clever they thought you were to speak such good English.'

We had reached the door. It swung open on silent hinges at the slightest pressure from the footman, and then we were back outside in the warm summer air.

The man who had brought us up from the jetty was waiting for us. He spoke to Basha Felika for a long time, and Basha Felika's eyebrows rose in surprise so high that they were almost lost in his hair.

At that moment a little carriage, pulled by a smart black pony, drew up. The driver wore a top hat and a long green coat and carried a whip in his hand.

'We *are* going up in the world,' Basha Felika said, lifting me into the carriage. 'Her Majesty has put this contraption at our disposal for the afternoon. We're going on a tour of the grounds.'

I think I'm a little better today. The fever has gone anyway, and my cough isn't quite so bad. I just feel very weak. Mrs Jex-Blake, the headmaster's wife, stood over me this morning with a bowlful of some kind of soup she'd told her cook to make. She wouldn't go away until I'd eaten a few spoonfuls. Perhaps the soup was a good idea after all, even though I hated having to eat it under Mrs Jex-Blake's cold eyes.

We stayed with some relatives of Basha Felika's on the Isle of Wight. We arrived at their house late in the afternoon. I shrank back into the carriage at the sound of barking dogs. Dogs in Abyssinia aren't like English dogs. People don't pet them and let them into their houses. Their job is to guard, and they'll attack anyone who comes near their master's property.

The two dogs bounding out of the house were the biggest I'd ever seen. They jumped up, barking noisily, their claws scratching against the door of the carriage.

'Bouncer! Nelson!' Basha Felika cried delightedly, and to my horror he opened the carriage door and jumped out. The dogs leaped up at him. I thought they were going to tear out his throat. I knew I ought to try to protect him, but I was too scared to move.

Basha Felika said something, and to my amazement the dogs dropped down and began to grovel at his feet, rolling over on to their backs.

'Rascals,' said Basha Felika.

I knew that word. I'd heard him use it on the ship when he talked about the sailors. He poked his head back into the carriage.

'Come on out, Alamayu. What are you waiting for?'

I swallowed hard. I was determined not to show fear.

You walked with lions, I told myself. These are only dogs.

Someone whistled and the dogs ran off towards a man coming out of the house. A moment later we were surrounded by people.

I don't remember much about those first weeks on the Isle of Wight. Basha Felika's relations were all big and hearty, with loud voices.

'Charlie!' they would call out to him. 'Char-lie!'

I tried it out on him myself the day after we arrived. 'Char-lee,' I said experimentally.

He laughed. 'You can call me Charlie if you like. It's not such a mouthful as Basha Felika, after all.'

So I called him Charlie after that, but in my heart of hearts he is still Basha, my captain, and Felika, my speedy one.

The house was quite small, and with so many large people, big dogs, Kassa and me it was crowded. It was awkward too, because the newspapers kept talking about me, and people were curious and wanted to see me. They would stand outside in the street and wait for me to appear. Some even knocked on the door and asked if they could see 'the little Abyssinian prince from Magdala'.

I didn't mind them much. It seemed normal. People always want to stare at princes. But it bothered Charlie.

'I can't turn round without some insolent beggar sticking his nose in my face,' he grumbled. 'I thought it would go off after a day or two, but it's getting worse and worse.'

An important man with a 'Sir' in front of his name even held a special party in his garden so that all his friends could look at me. Charlie groaned when the invitation came.

'We'll have to go and be stared at,' he said, 'Sorry, old chap. Needs must. Can't afford to offend the bigwigs.'

The Sir lived in a big house and there seemed to be hundreds of people already gathered when we arrived. We had to walk across the long lawn with all eyes on us. It was a bad moment for me. I felt like a freak. I held tightly to Basha Felika's hand. He was gripping mine too.

'It'll be all right,' he kept muttering to me. 'They're only trying to be friendly.'

I couldn't look at anyone. I wanted to shrink to nothing and disappear. I kept my eyes down and watched the caps on my boots going up and down, up and down, as I walked across the grass.

We went to Osborne again. I did as Charlie asked and let Kassa dress me in my old Abyssinian clothes. Charlie hummed and hawed and finally decided to dress up in his Abyssinian clothes too. We went in a closed carriage to Osborne, and people in the street didn't notice us. We drove through the lodge gates and up the big drive to the front door of the house, and the footmen in their scarlet coats and wigs hurried to open the door of the carriage and let down the steps. I saw their eyes widen in surprise at the sight of our strange clothes.

Charlie got his spear stuck in the carriage's upholstery, which annoyed the driver, and his long robes tangled in the carriage steps. I had to hold his shield while he arranged his lion-skin collar, refolded his *shamma* and set his cap straight on his head.

When we started to walk down that long corridor inside Osborne, with its noisy tiled floors, I was glad he was wearing his Abyssinian sandals instead of military boots. They didn't make such an embarrassing clatter.

The Queen and the princesses were in the same room as before, doing their sewing. I looked hopefully at the table, to see if there were any peaches, but there wasn't any fruit at all. The girls stared at Charlie and hid smiles behind their hands, but they cooed at me.

The Queen kissed me so I kissed her back, which she seemed to like, and then Princess Beatrice took me to a chair beside a small table and showed me some pictures in a book. I looked at them politely but they weren't very interesting – just scenes of mountains which were much smaller than our mountains at home. The table had a thick red cover on it with a fringe of bobbles. I started to play with them, but then I thought that might be impolite so I sat on my hands and leaned over the book again, kicking my feet against the bar of the chair and trying not to yawn.

Charlie and Queen Victoria were talking, and every now and then I heard my name and looked up. The Queen would smile at me and wave her hand.

'No peach today,' I said to Charlie as we stepped back out into the garden.

'What?' He didn't seem to have heard me.

'The Princess didn't give me a peach.'

'Oh, well. There you are, eh?'

I could tell that he still wasn't listening.

We stepped back into the carriage. Charlie sat in the corner, holding the strap in his hand and gazing silently out of the window. I began to feel worried. What had he been saying about me to the Queen? Was he telling her that he didn't want to look after me any more?

I decided to keep very quiet and not bother him. But then he heaved a big sigh and I felt such a shiver of fear that I blurted out, 'Are you cross with me, Charlie? Is it because I didn't bow to the Queen? Is she angry with me too?'

He brought his head round sharply to look at me. 'Angry with you? No. Why should I be?'

'I don't know. I – I thought . . .'

He smiled and squeezed my shoulder. 'The truth is, young Alamayu, that I wasn't thinking about you at all. I was thinking about – another – person altogether.'

I didn't like the sound of that. 'Who? What person? Is there another boy you want to take instead of me?'

He didn't take any notice of what I was saying, and I saw that his face was turning an interesting shade of deep red.

'I'm going to ask a . . . lady . . . if she will marry me,' he brought out at last.

'Oh!' I digested this. It sounded like bad news. 'Who is she?'

'Miss Cotton. You've met her. We went to her parents' house last week and the week before. She was the . . . the beautiful one who said she liked your new shoes.'

'Oh, yes. Her.'

I screwed up my eyes and tried to remember Miss Cotton. There had been so many visitors to the little house, and Charlie and I had called on so many people round the island, that it was hard to remember them all.

'If you get married,' I said, 'what's going to happen to me?'

He laughed. 'Is that what's worrying you? Well, you can put your mind at rest. The Queen wants you to stay with me. She was telling me so this afternoon. I'm to be your guardian. And if she – Miss Cotton – accepts me, you'll be living with her as well. She likes you. She told me so. We'll all be very happy together if . . .'

'If what, Charlie?'

He groaned.

'If she accepts my proposal.'

Charlie need not have worried. Miss Cotton did accept his proposal. When he told me, I felt a cold feeling inside, and then I wanted to do something bad, hit out at him, or even bite him. I hated the idea of anyone taking him away from me. I refused to look at Miss Cotton when Charlie took me to her house to visit, but then she did something that no one else in England had done.

'*Tenastelign*,' she said.

It was a greeting in Amharic, in my language. She had learned it for my sake.

Of course, my eyes then flew to her face, and I saw that she was looking at me seriously, her brown eyes fixed on mine as if I was a grown-up person. She didn't try to touch me or kiss me (I was tired of being pawed over by strangers). She stretched out her hand to show me the ring Charlie had given her.

'She wants me to tell you that this binds her to you as much as it does to me,' Charlie said.

I had to look away because of the sickly expression in his eyes and the syrupy tone in his voice.

If this is what getting married does to people, I told myself, I'm not going to do it. Ever.

Beetle came to see me this morning. I'm a bit stronger early in the day. The fever doesn't usually come until later in the afternoon.

He brought a jam jar with a little fish in it.

I tried to tell him that Nurse Thomson would tell him off, but for some reason I started laughing, and the laughing made me cough. Once I'd started, I couldn't stop. Beetle watched me anxiously until the coughing had passed, and I was lying back, exhausted, on the pillow.

'You've gone a funny colour,' he said. 'Sort of grey. Are you all right?'

I didn't answer. I didn't want to try speaking in case the coughing came back. Nurse Thomson put her head round the door.

'You'll have to go, young man, if you make him cough again,' she said severely.

'Let him stay,' I managed to croak.

Beetle sat in silence, staring at me anxiously. 'There's something I want to know, but not if you can't speak.'

'Go on,' I whispered.

He took a deep breath. 'I've been meaning to ask you for ages. It's just – I mean – can you remember seeing any insects . . . in Abyssinia?'

I was surprised. It took a moment for the question to sink in.

'Sorry,' he mumbled, looking more anxious than ever. 'I know you don't like talking about Abyssinia, but I really want to know.'

I tried to think.

'Fleas,' I managed to say at last, 'in the straw on the floor of the church. Lice. All the British soldiers had them. Mosquitoes, but not at Magdala. Only on the way down to the sea, where it was hot. Butterflies . . .'

I stopped.

He was leaning forward eagerly.

'Go on. What colour? How big?'

The effort of speaking was exhausting me.

'Don't remember.'

I shut my eyes. I could see the column of ants that had marched along the ground as my father's prisoners dragged themselves past in their clanking chains. I shut them out of my mind.

'A sort of beetle,' I whispered at last. 'They made balls out of cow dung and rolled them along the ground. They were really funny. I used to like watching them.'

He nodded.

'Dung beetles. I've read about them.' He cleared his throat. I had turned back to look at him, and was surprised to see a red flush of embarrassment creeping up his face.

'The thing is,' he went on, clasping his hands together between his knees, 'what I want to ask is, when you go back to Abyssinia, can I come too? On a scientific expedition, I mean. To collect insects.'

The thought was so absurd that I was in danger of laughing again. Only the fear of coughing stopped me. I didn't have to answer, because Nurse Thomson came bustling in.

'You've had long enough,' she said to Beetle. 'We don't want to tire the poor boy out, now, do we?'

I never gave Beetle an answer, but I've been thinking about what he said for hours.

When you go back to Abyssinia, he said.

Not if, but when.

I've daydreamed about going home, often enough, more than ever since I've been lying here, and Beetle has brought the dream closer. The idea of him, so solid, so strange and so British, walking through our mountains, along one of those narrow stony paths, is so peculiar that it makes me smile. But it warms my heart too. It brings my two selves, my Abyssinia and my England, closer together.

My heart warms at how he blushed when he brought out his request.

Beetle's visit has done me more good than a whole bottle full of medicine. He has made me think well of myself.

It wasn't long before I became used to the idea of Miss Cotton marrying Charlie. I had plenty of time to get acquainted with her. We visited the Cottons nearly every day once the engagement had been announced. Kassa and I would amuse each other while the other two would go for a walk.

Kassa was good at playing with me. He liked being in England, I think. He liked seeing things that were new and strange. He wanted to know how everything worked. Charlie had started giving me English lessons while we were staying with his relatives. Kassa used to listen. He couldn't read or write, even in Amharic, but he remembered English words almost as well as I did.

When we visited the Cottons, Charlie would say, 'Stay with Kassa, Alamayu. Miss Cotton and I are just going to walk into the village. We won't be long.'

I'd jump up and say, 'I'll come with you,' and Charlie would look at Kassa, who would take my hand and lead me to a bench by the wall of the house, beside a place where roses grew up over the old stones. I would start by going with him, then I'd snatch my hand away.

'I'm going to creep after Charlie and give him a surprise,' I'd say, but Kassa would shake his head.

'Better not, Prince. Anyway, let's practise our English.'

He would start strutting up and down the path with his chest stuck out, one arm held up as if he was holding a parasol. He'd pretend to catch sight of me.

'Eauw,' he'd say, copying old Mrs Cotton's English accent. 'Heow deu yiew deu?'

He would lean over to shake my hand.

'How you do too?' I'd say, vigorously pumping his.

'Heow yiew like dis countra?'

'Me like verra much.'

Then I'd revert to Amharic. 'I'll be the lady now, Kassa. You be me.'

Charlie and Miss Cotton always took much longer on their walks than I liked, and when they came back her cheeks were glowing pink. Miss Cotton was much shorter than Charlie. The top of her head only reached his shoulder.

'Tiny,' he called her.

'Why Tiny?' I asked him.

'It means "little" in English.'

'Same as Amharic,' I said, surprised. '"Little" is "*tinnish*".'

I liked Miss Cotton having a nearly Amharic name. I began calling her 'Tiny' too.

At the Cottons' house I didn't only play with Kassa. Her father and mother were always there. They were old of course, so they moved slowly and couldn't run about, but they liked me, and I liked them.

I wanted to go to the Cottons' house every morning. I was always ready before Charlie. I wanted only to escape his relatives' little house, with their big dogs and the windows so close to the road, through which strangers were always peering, trying to catch sight of me.

The Cottons' house had a big garden, like a park, with a wall all round it. No one could see us when we were inside it. There was a dog, but it was old, like its owners, and it was too lazy to bark or jump up. It would just stand, its tongue hanging out, waving its feathery tail.

I got used to it. I let it sniff me. I was soon happy to pat it and stroke its head. It liked that. The dog's name was Hercules. He wanted me to stroke him all the time.

There was something about the Cottons that made me love them. They seemed to understand me and know what kind of things I would like to do. Mr Cotton wore hairy tweed suits and he smelled of tobacco and soap. His white bushy eyebrows arched over his eyes, and his white bushy moustache drooped over his mouth. He spoke slowly and liked to make little jokes for me, producing pieces of barley sugar from an inside pocket, or making a coin appear from up his sleeve.

Mrs Cotton smelled of soap and her face was soft and pink. She thought a lot about giving people food. She considered that I was too small and thin for a boy of my age. She was always ringing a bell for a maid and asking her to bring me some biscuits and a glass of milk.

Mrs Cotton loved God and Jesus. She used to make Charlie ask me if I knew Bible stories, and when I showed her that I did she would smile and dab a tear away from her eye. She liked to hug me and stroke my cheek. I didn't mind much, but I preferred it when Mr Cotton sat me on his knee. It was too easy to sink right into Mrs Cotton and suffocate.

On my third or fourth visit I didn't feel the need to stick so closely to Charlie, and when he suggested going for a walk with Tiny to the end of the estate to admire the view, Mr Cotton scratched his ear and said something I didn't understand.

'Mr Cotton wants to know if you'd like to go to the stables with him to look at his horses,' Charlie translated for me.

I nodded eagerly. We set off, round the side of the house. As we went Mr Cotton was patting his pockets, checking that he had remembered to bring some sugar lumps.

I won't ever forget that morning. There were three horses looking out over the half-doors into the stable yard, and the stable boy was forking over a pile of hay with a pitchfork. Mr Cotton spoke to him, and he undid the latch on the door of one of the stalls and led out a small black pony, whose hoofs clattered on the stones of the stable yard.

'Blackie – his name's Blackie,' said Mr Cotton.

I watched while the boy saddled Blackie. Then suddenly I found myself being swung up into the air, and I was landed on Blackie's back.

I felt – I don't know why – a wild joy. It was a kind of homecoming for me. Mr Cotton nodded at the boy (his name was Joe), and the boy took hold of Blackie's reins and began to lead him slowly round the yard, but I pulled the rein away from him and dug my heels into the pony's sides to make him trot.

'*Hid!*' I shouted, as we did in Abyssinia. 'Go on! *Hid!*'

There was a laugh from behind me. Charlie and Tiny had come into the yard. Charlie caught at the reins as I rode past him for the fourth time.

'Enough for one day,' he said. 'Mrs Cotton says that lunch is ready.'

'Can I ride him tomorrow? Will you ask my *wond eyat*?' I begged, using the Amharic expression for 'Grandfather'.

Charlie laughed. 'Grandfather, is it now? You'd better learn to say it in English. "Grandpapa".'

'Grant-puppa,' I said. 'Please – horse – again.'

'Did he call me "Grandpapa"?' Mr Cotton said to Charlie. 'Well now. Well.'

I could tell he was pleased, though he tried not to show it. He tugged at the side of his moustache, then pulled some sugar lumps out of his pocket and gave them to me.

'For Blackie,' he said. 'You do it. Tomorrow we'll bring him some more.'

At tea, when Mrs Cotton heard me talk to Mr Cotton, she said, '"Grandpapa", is it? Then you must call me Grandmamma.' And I did from then on.

Charlie and Tiny were married in December, but he and I moved into Afton Manor, the Cottons' big house, months earlier, when it was still high summer.

Afton Manor. It's floating there, before my closed eyes. Charlie takes me down to the sea and teaches me to swim while Tiny stands on the shore holding a towel to wrap me in when I emerge shivering from the water. Steaming dishes of food cover the long table in the dining room, and I eat everything, the fasting rules of my own religion long forgotten. As autumn turns to winter I watch in dismay

On the Isle of Wight

as the leaves fall, fearing that the trees are dying, but Tiny shows me the little buds at the end of each twig and tells me that they will sprout when spring comes. As the days grow dark and cold, fires are lit in the house, and after riding out with Grandpapa, I flop down on the hearthrug beside Hercules, who yawns and thumps his tail on the floor. It's my turn to yawn in the mornings, when Charlie tries to teach me English letters. He never threatens to beat me, and I do my best for him. Soon I know the whole alphabet by heart. I start to understand more and more English words and then find I can catch most of what people are saying, and answer them a bit too.

I'm too busy in my new life to spend much time with Kassa. He looks colder and less happy as the winter advances. The Cottons have hired a nursery maid for me. Her name is Louisa. She understands that I'm a prince and treats me correctly.

But the nights! Oh, the nights are still hard, even here at Afton Manor, surrounded by peace and by people who want to help me. I can never go to sleep unless Charlie is with me, his strong arm surrounding me. Terrors crowd in on me. Nightmarish faces. Blazing guns. Screams. The bodies of the dead and dying.

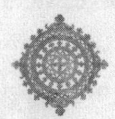

I was a groomsman at Charlie and Tiny's wedding. I had to follow Charlie up the aisle and walk behind the bride and groom in the procession from the church to the Manor, surrounded by the bridesmaids in their big puffy dresses. I looked nice in my velvet suit. Everyone smiled at me and some people tried to pat my head. I disliked that, but thought it would be undignified to dodge them, so I put up with it, only showing by my frown that I would prefer not to be touched by strangers.

I'm not a dog, I wanted to say to them. Please keep at a proper distance.

At the wedding breakfast, after the toasts had been drunk to the bride and groom, the toastmaster said, 'Ladies and gentlemen, pray raise your glasses to Prince Alamayu of Abyssinia.'

I knew what I had to do. I had watched Charlie and Tiny. I stood up and said, 'Me tank you verra much.'

It had gone down well with Queen Victoria and the princesses. It caused a sensation at the wedding breakfast. Everyone said, 'Ahh,' and then they clapped.

I knew that Charlie and Tiny were going off on their wedding tour, but I watched them leave with my heart in my mouth. That night I woke sobbing and gasping from a nightmare. Louisa was there, sleeping as she always did in a bed beside mine.

'Take me into your bed, Louisa!' I cried. 'Satan is holding me. He is so bad! So bad!'

In the morning, when I went into the dining room for breakfast, Grandpapa lowered his newspaper and looked at me from under his beetling white brows.

'Had a bad night, did we, old fellow? Let's go and see Blackie. He needs to go out for a ride.'

We stayed with the Cottons at Afton Manor for nearly a year. It's strange, but I don't remember much about those times except that I was happy.

Kassa left after a while. He had become more and more silent and sad, until finally Charlie could bear his long face no more and booked him a passage on a ship leaving Portsmouth for Suez. I hardly noticed his departure. I didn't want to speak Amharic any more. I was too busy being spoiled, I suppose, by my new family. I only wanted to become one of them.

There was one thing, though that I did mind about Kassa's departure. No one but him had truly understood my royalty. No one else, not even Charlie, had known the awe and terror that Father cast around him. No one but Kassa saw me as his heir.

It was only once I had learned some English that I fully realized that the title had been dropped from my name. In Abyssinia I was 'Dejazmatch Alamayu'. In England I was only ever Alamayu.

'Why don't the English call me "Prince"?' I asked Charlie, when some children in the town of Cowes, chanting my name, had particularly annoyed me.

I caught the look that he exchanged with Tiny. I saw that my question had made them both uncomfortable.

'What's in a name?' he said lightly, making a fist and playfully punching my shoulder.

For once I was angry with him. 'A king's son is always a prince,' I said stiffly, and I refused to talk to him for the rest of the day.

They must have seen more clearly than I could how empty my title had become. What is a prince, after all, without a homeland, or a retinue of servants, or a living king and queen for his father and mother?

Blackie and I went hunting together, cantering through the lanes and across the fields of the Isle of Wight. Did I think, on those wild dashes across the countryside, as the hounds bayed ahead of us and Grandpapa rode beside me on his steady grey hunter, of Father galloping on Hamra at the head of his cavalry? I don't think I did. Abyssinia was fading fast, like the morning mist under a rising sun.

Your mind plays funny tricks on you when there's nothing much for it to do. I think it was the words 'grandfather' and 'grandmother' that have made me think of something strange that happened here in Rugby last term.

The chancellor of Great Britain is the person who makes decisions about me. He's in charge of my future and my life here in England. Every now and then, someone comes to Rugby from London, sent by the chancellor, to see how I'm getting on and to discuss what is to be done with me. I know when such a person is coming because I'm called to the headmaster's study to be interviewed.

Last time he came I was in a maths class, and Mr Hutchinson was droning on in a voice that was sending me to sleep. A boy from the lower school put his head round the door.

'Please, sir – Alamayu is to go at once to the headmaster's study.'

Mr Hutchinson frowned, sighed, said, 'What have you done this time, boy? I suppose you'd better go.'

I had known someone was coming to see me so I wasn't afraid. 'Thank you, sir,' I said, and hurried out of the classroom.

Dr Jex-Blake's study door was half open. I paused outside it. Through the crack, I could see the visitor's back and the grey hair fringing his bald head as he sat in a chair in front of the headmaster's desk. He spoke in a dry, clipped voice. It wasn't anyone I had met before.

'There's been a letter. For the prince.'

I had been about to knock and go in, but I stood frozen,

listening as hard as I could. There was a rustling noise and I imagined Dr Jex-Blake pushing the sleeves of his black gown back as he leaned forward across his desk.

'Really? Who from?'

'We don't know for sure. It's in Amharic, or whatever their lingo's called. No one can read it. The courier who brought it says it's probably from the grandmother.'

'Alamayu has a grandmother?'

'So it would seem. His mother's mother, apparently. How is the boy?'

'Well enough. He's popular. Very well liked by the other boys.'

'Making progress with his studies?'

'Barely. He's perfectly intelligent. He could do well, but he's a dreamer. He seems to be elsewhere half the time. Very hard to get him to concentrate.'

'Pity.'

There was a short silence. I heard the clink of china and guessed the visitor was sipping from a cup.

When Dr Jex-Blake next spoke he sounded defensive. 'We do our best with him, you know, but he won't put his mind to anything in class. My staff are very good.'

'Of course.'

Another silence. Then Dr Jex-Blake said, 'What are we to do about this letter? Do you have it with you?'

There was a crackle of paper.

'Good heavens!' Dr Jex-Blake sounded startled. 'Is that Amharic script? I've never seen anything like it.'

The paper rustled again. I imagined the headmaster turning it over, and holding it up to his eyes.

'What do you want us to do with it?' he said at last, a little irritably. 'What does it say?'

'That's just the trouble. We don't know.'

'Can't you get one of your people in the Foreign Office to translate it?'

Dr Jex-Blake

''Fraid not. The only person we know of who can read this stuff is Captain Speedy, and he, as you know, is abroad.'

'Speedy! The last person we want meddling round here again, upsetting the boy, putting ideas into his head.'

'The chancellor's thought precisely. However, we should perhaps give the letter to the Prince. It's addressed to him, after all. I believe he learned to read Amharic as a child.'

'There's no point, my dear sir. He forgot all that a long time ago. I don't suppose he remembers a word of his mother tongue now. I think, you know, that it would be best to say nothing about this. Take the thing back to London. Someone'll show up in due course who can decipher it.'

'Are you sure? It seems . . . not quite . . . right – to withhold it from the boy.'

'It's the best course, I assure you. Let sleeping dogs lie. No point in stirring up the past. Alamayu's an English schoolboy now. I'm sure he never gives Abyssinia a thought.'

I could hold myself back no longer. I knocked on the door, and without waiting for the usual peremptory 'Come!' from the headmaster, pushed it wide open and went inside.

The visitor twisted round in his chair to look at me.

'Prince Alamayu?'

'Yes, sir.'

He seemed nonplussed and looked across to Dr Jex-Blake for guidance. I let my eyes fall as if casually on the letter that the headmaster had laid down on the desk.

'That looks like Amharic, sir. May I see?'

Before either of them could move, I had darted forward and picked it up. My hand shook as I stared down at those small black characters, at once so familiar and so strange.

'Is this a letter for me?' I asked innocently. 'From home?'

The visitor cleared his throat. 'So it would seem. You can read it?'

'I – no. I . . . I've forgotten how to.'

Out of the corner of my eye I could see Dr Jex-Blake give a triumphant little nod.

'It appears that someone in Abyssinia has remembered you, Alamayu, and has sent you this letter, but as you cannot read it I see no purpose in your retaining it. Give it to me.'

'It's . . . It's mine, sir,' I said, summoning up my courage.

The visitor coughed. 'If I may be permitted to make a suggestion. Allow me to return to London with this letter, prince, where I will attempt to find someone who can translate it for you. It will then be returned to you so that you can read it.'

I shut my eyes for a moment. It was years since I had thought of my grandmother. I barely remembered the old woman who had stayed sometimes with us in the King's House, plaiting Amma's hair, sighing over lost relatives, calling to Abebech to bring her a *shamma*.

The letter seemed to burn my fingers. I raised it to my face and breathed in a faint scent of incense and woodsmoke. What choice did I have? Desperate as I was to keep the letter, I knew that my only chance of ever knowing what it said was to return it to the visitor.

'Please,' I said to him, as I handed it back. 'do your best for me, sir. Please.'

I waited, week after week, for a letter from London with a translation of my grandmother's words. It never came. I suppose I forgot about it after a while. Now I wonder more and more insistently about what she was trying to tell me. If – when – I go home, she's the first person I shall look for. There'll be no need for words. Just to look into her face will be enough for me.

I suppose I was living in a fool's paradise during that long happy time staying with the Cottons. Now I come to think of it, Charlie must have started to feel restless. He was a soldier, after all, used to being active and to having men under his command. He loved the outdoors life, sleeping in tents, travelling on campaign, making do with very little. He loved the glamour of the parades, the spectacle of marching men in their scarlet uniforms, the bands playing, the flags flying, the horses obedient to the strident bugle calls. I'm sure his men respected and trusted him.

He was never impatient with me as he taught me my English lessons in the morning. He wasn't a very good teacher. He spent too much time looking out of the window at Tiny, sitting under a parasol beside her mother.

We became quite used to visiting the Queen at Osborne. The cold marble statues in the corridors no longer frightened me, and I was happy to run along to the little room where the Queen usually sat, or, on fine days, out to the terrace with its view of the sea and the white sails bending in the breeze. I always hoped that Princess Beatrice would be there, and that she would take me to ride in her pony cart.

The Queen always smiled at me and called me her 'dear little friend'. She liked to hug and kiss me, but it wasn't a comfortable feeling. The silk of her dress was shiny and cold and there was a brooch with a picture of her dead husband stuck on it, which threatened to scratch my face.

To my mind, Father was much more like a real monarch, sitting in state surrounded by his lords and officers in their golden embroideries, his eyes darting round the audience hall, his lions at his feet. No one dared to look at him. It was Queen Victoria, though, who frightened Charlie, more than Father had ever done. His voice sounded tight and squeaky whenever he spoke to her.

In the end, of course, Charlie had to move on from the Isle of Wight. He couldn't dance attendance on me forever. His next posting came through one summer morning, carried up to the house by the whistling postman, who had become my friend.

'It's to be India,' Charlie said to Tiny, who was still at the breakfast table. She was gripping the handle of her teacup so hard I thought it might snap off. 'Superintendent of police in a town called Sitapur in the district of Oudh. Run along to the library, Alamayu, and fetch me the atlas. Let's find out where it is we're going.'

It's quite interesting to think about how my life might have turned out if things had been different. The best thing of all would have been a life at home with Amma in the King's House in Magdala, with my parents happy and well and loving each other, and never angry any more. In this impossible dream, Father's enemies would all be defeated, and the British would be our friends and allies. I would be Father's crown prince, his heir, learning to be his successor, at some far-distant date.

Since that life is closed to me, I would have liked to remain as Charlie's and Tiny's boy, listening to Charlie's marvellous stories, showing Tiny my cuts and bruises, then wriggling away from her kisses, following Charlie on his strange career to India and Malaya and beyond.

I would never have chosen to be taken away from them, and from everyone I had ever known. I never wanted to be an English schoolboy.

It's not that I don't like it here at Rugby. It's all right. I'm popular now, I know I am, and I have really good friends, but even to Beetle and Bull I'm a strange creature, exotic, with no family, no roots, no place in their world. To most of the others I look like the pictures of slaves and savages they see in books, even though they know that I'm a prince. And to myself? Who am I? I wish I knew.

The chancellor and the grey men from government departments are my only parents now.

They didn't let me stay with Charlie. My life with him and Tiny was over from one day to the next.

'They want you to stay in England,' Charlie said, holding the letter close to his short-sighted eyes and running a hand across his unruly red hair, as he always did when he was agitated. 'They think you ought to have a proper English education.'

'Oh,' I said, rather pleased at the idea. I was too stupid to realize what this meant. I was thinking of some boys I'd played with once or twice on the Isle of Wight during their school holidays. They described jolly tricks they had played on their school friends, and exciting outings to London with the uncle and aunt who looked after them sometimes.

Then a thought struck me.

'Charlie! You don't mean that they want me to stay in England on my own?'

'Not if I have anything to do with it!' Tiny had jumped out of her chair and was holding out her hand to read the letter. 'They can't take you away from us now! The Queen won't let them!' She ran her eyes quickly down the page.

Charlie took it from her again. 'This says that my guardianship has been terminated!' He was peering closely at the letter, his face red with indignation. 'I'm to set sail immediately, and I'm to hand Alamayu over to a –' he peered closely at the letter – 'a Dr Jex-Blake, whoever he is.'

I felt my stomach falling.

'You can't, Charlie!' I wailed. 'I won't stay! You can't just leave me here!'

'Of course we won't!' Tiny gave me one of her quick hugs. 'Charlie, you must start writing letters. To Sir Thomas Biddulph, the chancellor, the Queen, to everyone! Anyway, I'm sure the Jex-Blakes won't want him right away. We'll have time to make them change their minds.'

The next few weeks were horrible. Tiny fretted over me, while Mrs Cotton tried to make her gather the things she would need for her new life in the tropics. At the small desk in the library Charlie laboured over letters, muttering angrily as he wrote. He would pace up and down when the postman was expected, and run out to meet him. I had never seen him so disturbed. Sometimes he would go over to the mainland to stay there for days.

I went with him from time to time. We were summoned to Brighton to meet important men from the government, then to Windsor to see the Queen. I was taken to see Mr Gladstone in Downing Street, where two doctors examined me.

Charlie's anxiety infected me too.

'What's going to happen to me?' I kept asking him. 'Why can't I go with you?'

I thought, but didn't dare say out loud, 'Don't you and Tiny want me any more?'

I was dimly aware of the tug of war going on over my head. One morning I overheard Charlie reading out a letter to Tiny, his voice hoarse with indignation.

'Listen to this! That monstrous man at the Treasury writes to tell me that he is *tired* of all the *cant* over Alamayu. He rants on that education doesn't consist in *coddling* or *petting* children, if you please, but in making *men* of them. And how do you think he proposes to make a man of Alamayu? The boy's to be thrown into the bear pit of a public school, without a home of his own to go to in the holidays!'

'Hush, my dear,' Tiny said, seeing my shocked face as I stood and listened at the door. 'You'll frighten Alamayu to death. Come here, darling.' I went to her, and she put an arm around my shoulders and squeezed them. 'You mustn't worry. We won't ever let you go.'

But you did let me go, Tiny. You and Charlie had no choice. Not even Queen Victoria could change the minds of those grey men in the Treasury. You were packed off overseas, and they gave me to Dr Jex-Blake. I know you wanted to keep me. I know you fought for me. But couldn't you have tried harder? If you had insisted, wouldn't you have won in the end?

Dr Jex-Blake wasn't yet at Rugby when I was handed over to him like a bundle of washing. He was the headmaster of another school, in Cheltenham. I shrank inside myself, back to that place of cold stillness which I thought had melted forever, when Charlie and I stepped out of the train at Cheltenham. We stood in a biting cold March wind waiting for a hackney cab to take us to the school.

A maid opened the door to us. I saw my new teacher and guardian for the first time. His clergyman's collar was half hidden by his long side whiskers. He held out a hand to Charlie with a jovial smile, which didn't extend to his eyes.

'Well,' he said, laying a heavy hand on my shoulder, 'so this is our young man.'

'This is *Prince* Alamayu,' Charlie said stiffly.

'Oh, we won't fuss over titles here,' said Dr Jex-Blake. 'Alamayu will be part of our family, won't you, my boy?'

Charlie, taken by a sudden panic, took hold of my arm and backed nervously down the steps away from the door.

'We . . . We only came to make sure we had found the correct house,' he said. 'I've ordered dinner at my hotel for Alamayu and me. Our last evening together, you see. We . . . would like to spend it together.'

'Nonsense!' cried Dr Jex-Blake, taking hold of my shoulder again and almost dragging me away from Charlie. 'No point in prolonging farewells. Dine with us if you choose, sir, but our instructions from the Treasury are clear. The boy is in my charge now.'

The two men stared at each other over my head. I sensed a battle of wills raging through the polite silence.

It was Mrs Jex-Blake who fired the winning shot. She turned to the array of daughters standing behind her.

'Lucy,' she said, her stiff cheeks creased in a polite smile. 'Go upstairs with Alamayu and show him where he is to sleep. Evangeline, take Captain Speedy's hat. Violet, instruct the cab driver to fetch in Alamayu's belongings, and Henrietta, tell Cook to bring forward dinner immediately.'

I can't say that the Jex-Blakes have ever been cruel to me exactly. It's just that I'm a duty to them. They never loved me, as Charlie and Tiny had done. They've never hugged me, like Tiny did, or said, 'Oh, Alamayu, what a funny boy you are.' They've never wrestled with me, and made me laugh, like Charlie used to. When I think of Dr Jex-Blake I see him frowning and hear him saying, 'Got to stand on your own two feet, my boy,' or, 'You must apply yourself, Alamayu, or you'll never get on.'

The worst thing they did was refuse to allow Tiny to visit me, though later I learned that she had stayed behind in England for months, just to be near me. How was I to know that? No one explained things to me. I thought that Tiny didn't want to bother with me any more.

Those nine big Jex-Blake daughters seemed to buffet and crush me. At breakfast time they made two long rows down the sides of the table, with Dr Jex-Blake at one end, solemnly saying grace, and Mrs Jex-Blake at the other, signalling to the maid to bring more hot water. I was never hungry. I would fiddle with the white tablecloth which fell down on to my knees and refuse to eat my egg.

I would turn round at any sound from outside, especially when I heard the clop of hoofs and the squeak of carriage springs from the road outside, hoping desperately that Tiny would come and rescue me. I knew there was no hope of seeing Charlie. He had sailed weeks earlier.

They made me work all day. Reading, writing, Latin, English, arithmetic – the little figures and numbers jumbled themselves together on the pages of the horrid books and made a sort of mist in my head. I would look out of the window as often as I could, hoping to hear the postman, and when the letter box in the hall rattled I would make an excuse to leave the room and try to get to the front door before the maid had a chance to pick the letters up. She always got there first.

'Isn't there anything for me, Ellen?' I would ask her.

She wouldn't even look at the sheaf of letters in her hand.

'I dunno, Master Alamayu. The doctor'll tell you if there is.'

There were letters for me. I know there were. I often recognized Tiny's elegant handwriting before Ellen carried them away.

I think it was Queen Victoria herself who commanded Mrs Jex-Blake to let Tiny visit me. I didn't wonder then, how this great Queen, who ruled over such a vast empire, could find the time to worry about me, but she did. I love her for that kindness.

When Tiny came at last I hung back, feeling
shy.

'Alamayu, dearest!' she cried, swooping on me, v
Mrs Jex-Blake stood by disapprovingly. 'My darling boy.
You've grown! And – so thin!'

Mrs Jex-Blake took in a sharp breath. 'His meals are
perfectly adequate, I assure you, Mrs Speedy.'

Tiny knew better than to antagonize her further. She
turned on her a pretty smile.

'Of *course*! I'm *sure*! It's just that – as you can imagine –
I've been so anxious to see him after all this time.'

'Three weeks, I believe. Hardly a long time.'

I stared at Mrs Jex-Blake open-mouthed. Had I been
lost in this forest of girls for only three weeks?

I don't remember how Tiny managed it, but a little while
later she had extracted me from the house and my day's
lessons and we were walking together away from the school.

'Oh, my poor boy! Is it too awful?' Tiny's arm was
round my shoulders and she gave me a squeeze.

'It's all right,' I said gruffly.

Why couldn't I tell Tiny how miserable I was? I had begun
to bar her from my inner self. I even wanted to wriggle
out from under her arm. A voice inside me was saying, You
abandoned me to these people. How can I trust you any more?

At the end of an awkward afternoon it was almost
a relief to say goodbye to Tiny. I stood stiffly as she bent

kiss me, watched once more by Mrs Jex-Blake.

'I'll go on writing to you every day,' she said.

My eyes flew up to her face.

'Every day? But . . .'

'And you'll write to me?'

Mrs Jex-Blake broke in with a shrill little laugh. 'You'll be hard put to it to get a letter out of Alamayu.' She pinched my cheek. 'We don't like writing much, do we? Mrs Speedy, I can assure you that Alamayu has every facility for writing letters, but there appears to be no one he cares to write to.'

Tiny gasped and put a hand up to her throat. I wriggled with embarrassment between them.

It was easier the second time Tiny came, but something in my heart had closed against her. I had trusted Charlie and Tiny as if they had been my true parents. I felt they had abandoned me.

Tiny took me to a tea shop in Cheltenham and tried to feed me with cakes.

'I'm not hungry,' I said, pushing my plate away.

She put her hand on mine.

'You're not happy, dear. Tell me.'

I cast a swift look round the tea shop. Everyone was staring at me and I could see that they were trying to listen to us as well. I pulled my hand away from hers.

'I'm all right,' I said miserably.

As we left the tea shop I saw a woman nudge her

companion and whisper, 'I told you. It *is* him! The Abyssinian prince!'

I understood after she'd gone that I would have to live without Tiny and Charlie from now on. My path had parted from theirs. I was in the charge of Dr and Mrs Jex-Blake, and when he came to be the headmaster of Rugby, I came here too.

The entrance to Rugby School

I think I must be feeling a little better. My eyes don't hurt so much when I try to move them, and I don't mind eating a little of the jelly Nurse Thomson keeps offering me. The fever seems to be going off at last.

I'm glad, of course. I want to get better. But now that the fever has left, my memories of Abyssinia have left with it. They were so bright and sharp that I felt I was that funny child again, running about the mountain top in my bare feet, and that Father and Amma were really there, along with Gebre, and Abebech, and Mr Rassam, and Charlie, and everyone else I knew and loved. They've slipped away, back into the past, hidden behind a curtain.

I'm glad I've had the chance to live through those years again. I can make more sense of them now. They've reminded me of who I am. They've given me a new ambition – to go home, one day, and enter my inheritance.

How long have I been at Rugby? Two years, or is it three? Sometimes I feel that I've been here forever.

Those first months are a jumble in my mind now, a confused blur of big fellows rushing about, and stuffy classrooms, and bruises after football, and feeling lost, and being lonely, and trying not to show that I was frightened.

It was all much, much better after I made friends with Beetle. Without him, I'd never have been able to stand up to Carson.

Ivor Carson. Somehow I know that I won't get better until I've dealt with him.

Once Carson had begun to take notice of me, he didn't leave me alone. He always wanted the same thing: to make me talk about Abyssinia and my father. The boys surrounding him thought he was being kind to me. Sometimes I even thought so myself. Usually, though, I felt the rapier thrust hidden behind his smooth words. The other boys, who were always hanging around him, didn't seem to notice or didn't care how sharply his dagger struck.

'Come here, young Alamayu,' he called out to me one day as I was hurrying out of chapel. I obeyed, of course. Everyone obeyed Carson. 'Have you been to the British Museum yet? The Magdala treasure's on show. Your father's crowns, lots of books and pictures and some rather jolly crosses. My old man took me there in the holidays. He brought a few things back from Abyssinia himself. One of them's a nice gold bracelet. He's having it altered so Mama can wear it. You should go to the British Museum and see it all. I'm sure you'd love it.'

I put my hands behind my back so that no one could see how hard I was gripping them together. He waited for me to say something, but I couldn't have uttered a word.

'Are you playing football this term?'

'I hope so.'

'I'll watch out for you. See how you're shaping up. They tell me you show promise.'

Boys crowded round me when he'd passed on his way.

'What did Carson say to you? He'll watch out for you? You lucky devil. I'd give anything for him to say that to me.'

I didn't answer them. I was looking down at the palm of my left hand. The nails of my right hand had dug into it so hard they had left deep dents.

Beetle was standing behind them. I pushed my way through to him.

'Prat,' he said under his breath.

The blood that had rushed to my head was still buzzing in my ears.

'What did you say?'

'Carson – a prat. The looting of Magdala. It was theft. Pure robbery. My father said so anyway.'

At that moment I would have died for Beetle.

Carson sometimes tried to goad me into talking about Abyssinia. He wasn't the only person, of course, who did so. I never wanted to.

'What's it like, being in a battle?' someone would say. 'I'm going into the army as soon as I leave school.'

'It was years ago,' I'd answer. 'I've forgotten all about it.'

Once or twice, though, I was pushed into saying more than I wanted to.

'I suppose they're all heathens in Abyssinia, aren't they?' one ignorant boy said. 'It's Africa, isn't it?'

I couldn't stand for that.

'Abyssinia's the oldest Christian country in the world,' I blurted out. 'We were Christians long before the English.'

He didn't believe me, of course. He made a funny face and he and his friend ran off laughing.

Beetle happened to be there. He stood looking after the boy, then turned back to me, frowning.

'I never asked you anything about Abyssinia, or what happened to you – before. I suppose you had a hard time. You must think I'm stupid or I don't care or something. I don't mind if you do want to talk about all that sort of thing.'

I shuddered.

'I don't! I don't want to talk about it at all! I can't help remembering things sometimes, but I'd much rather forget. I *can* forget when I'm with you.'

'Good. All right then. Where are you off to, anyway?'

'I don't know. What about you?'

'Down to the meadow. Saw a swallowtail butterfly there last week. Couldn't understand it. Much too early in the year. Are you coming?'

'I'll come,' I said.

We set off across the football field towards the row of trees at the far end. Just before we reached them, he said, 'There are a couple of things I want to ask you. You don't have to tell me, but I hear fellows saying things and I don't know how to answer them. I can shut them up if I know the truth.'

'Go on,' I said cautiously.

'Some of them said your father was mad. Crazy. Is that true?'

'No! He was a great king. And a genius.'

'I thought so. They call me a lunatic and I'm not, so I guessed they were wrong about him too.'

'What's the other question?'

'Did you – he – your father . . . really have tame lions? Did you ride on them?'

'Yes. There was one, called Gobezu . . .' I stopped.

'Oh!' He stopped and stared at me, his eyes wide open. 'I thought that must be just a story.'

I looked away from him, across the meadow. 'Can we stop talking about it now, Beetle? I don't want to, even to you.'

He moved the shaft of the butterfly net from one shoulder to the other.

'Nothing more I want to say. Here, do you mind carrying this specimen box? I'll need my hands free if I do see a swallowtail. I'll have to go for it at once.'

Football is very important at Rugby. The way we play it is spreading now to other schools. Being captain of football is just about the most important thing you can be, and it's one reason why everyone treats Carson with such respect.

I love playing football. I'm good at it too. The first time I did really well was when our house, Elsee's, played School House. It was a cold day in October. I shivered in my striped jersey and thin trousers and puffs of steam rose from my mouth when I breathed out. As I waited for the ball to come my way I jumped up and down to keep warm and slapped my hands against my chest. But after a couple of good runs I was as hot as if it had been a sunny day in June.

I'm a switcher. I stand beside the scrimmage, every sense alert, my cap rammed down on my head. The ball flies out and I dart in. With a leap, I intercept it. Then I'm off, running down the Big Side, dodging and twisting, as

The football field at Rugby School

fast as a gazelle, until one of the fellows on the other side catches me round the waist and another hurls himself at my ankles and I'm down under a mass of them. But before I fall, if I'm lucky, I've passed the ball to one of our men, and on he goes. The boys peel off me and I stagger to my feet, pick up my cap and gasp for breath as I watch with narrowed eyes for the next chance, ready to leap in again.

I played a good game that day. I helped our win. People were watching us from behind the try line, even a couple of masters. They looked like big crows, with their black gowns on their backs and their mortar boards on their heads.

'We ought to have had reserve players to come on fresh when our men got tired,' I heard the School House captain say to one of his team, as they walked, tired and beaten, off the field.

'Yes, but what we really need is a good switcher,' someone answered.

'An Alamayu,' someone else chipped in.

'That's right,' nodded the captain. 'An Alamayu.'

They hadn't seen me. They weren't trying to flatter me. I snatched my cap off my head and threw it into the air.

Then Carson, surrounded by his usual band of followers, sauntered past.

'Good playing,' he shouted at me, 'for a black man!'

Everyone else thought he was praising me, but I heard only his contempt.

Things with Carson might have rumbled on forever, never coming to a head, if it hadn't been for the Rugby School Volunteer Corps. Being in the Volunteer Corps is the first step towards being an officer in the army.

I'd known, ever since I'd watched General Napier parade his troops at Senafe, that the army would one day be the place for me, but I hadn't given it much thought.

I joined the corps almost by accident. I'd planned to go out with Beetle, but he'd fallen over a dead branch lying hidden in the long grass on the meadow and had sprained his ankle. I'd taken him back to school and left him with Nurse Thomson.

As I was coming out of the door into the quad, I met the Volunteer Corps marching back from their rifle practice. They were wearing their uniforms. I thought they looked good.

Bulliver (the boy we call Bull) was taller than all the others. He stood out like an eagle among a flock of pigeons.

'Hey, Alamayu,' he shouted out. 'Why don't you join us? You'd make a first-class soldier. We do drills and learn how to shoot. It's the best fun.'

I'd always liked Bull, but we didn't know each other well. It was only later that we became good friends. I wasn't scared of him, like some of the others were. He was

big and charged about the place, but I could always tell that
he didn't mean any harm.

His friendliness cheered me and I smiled, standing back
to let him pass.

'I don't know,' I said.

'You'd love it,' Bull called back over his shoulder. 'We
need good fellows like you.'

I took a deep breath. I'd been a child for too long,
watching from the side as Father rode out at the head of
his cavalry, and General Napier paraded his troops in front
of the Abyssinian chiefs, and the Grenadier Guards in their
bearskins marched up and down in front of one of Queen
Victoria's great houses.

'All right,' I said, to Bull's departing back, too quietly
for him to hear. 'I'll volunteer.'

I didn't hesitate after that. Even though it was the British
who invaded my country and caused my father's death, I'd
never really thought of them as my enemies. I'm more like
a British boy than an Abyssinian prince now anyway.

A week later I was kitted out in the uniform of a private
in the 3rd Warwickshire Rifle Volunteers. We have to wear
blue coats with Austrian knots in dark braid across the
front. The shako has a peak to keep the sun out of our eyes,
and a pompom sticks up from the top. The badge pinned to
the front of the shako is a little silver model of a galloping
stag with antlers.

We have to keep our things very smart. The officers

inspect us when we go on parade. Everything has to be perfect. Our shoes must gleam without a speck of dust, our belts must be polished, our jackets must be brushed and our trousers pressed without a crease.

It's easier for me to do everything right than it is for some of the others. I spent long enough with Basha Felika to learn how a soldier has to behave. The sergeant never has to take my name for being improperly dressed.

I wish that Father could see me in my uniform, learning how to be a proper soldier. I know that he would have approved. He wanted me to learn the customs of the British. He admired the way they ran their army. I can imagine how his eyes would have narrowed as he watched us. He would have assessed our strength, trying to judge our fighting power. He would have liked to see the rifles we use too. He was always interested in technical things — in machines, especially modern weapons.

What would Amma have thought if she'd seen me in my British uniform? Would she have been shocked, sad, angry or even a little proud? There's no one I can ask.

It was thanks to the Volunteer Corps that I made another friend, after a shaky start. I first met him when I was on my way to drill practice, dodging over the puddles and taking

care not to get mud on my boots before inspection. A boy
I hadn't seen before trotted up alongside me. He ran in a
jerky way, his legs buckling a bit at the knees.

'Hello, Blackie,' he said. My heart kicked with anger
but he didn't notice my scowl. 'Are you in the corps? Are
you going to the range?'

'And hello to you, Funny-legs,' I said. 'Yes, that's where
I'm going.'

He looked shocked and threw an anxious glance over
his shoulder.

'Hey, don't call me that. The other boys might hear.
They'll all start.'

'I won't call you Funny-legs if you don't call me Blackie.
It's a good name for a horse. It's not a name for me.'

'I'm sorry. I didn't mean . . . Anyway, there's nothing
funny about my legs.'

I studied them. 'If you say so. But you can't call my face
black, exactly, either.'

He looked properly at me for the first time. 'Well, it's
actually a sort of reddish brown colour. Look, my name's
Peter. Peter Simpson.'

'All right, Simpson. I'm Alamayu.'

'Alam what?'

'Don't worry. You can call me Ali.' *Or Prince*, I said
silently to myself.

It was as if I had spoken out loud. His eyebrows flicked
together in thought.

'Aren't you a prince or something? I heard one of them say something about it.'

'My father was a king, so, yes, I am a prince.'

'Wait a minute.' I could almost see the wheels in his brain turning. 'Wasn't your father that –' he was about to say 'crazy' but stopped himself in time – 'the one we . . . we went to war with in Abyssinia?'

I sighed. 'You're new at the school then?' I said, hoping to divert him from asking any tiresome questions.

'Yes. Is it true that . . . ?'

At that moment there was a shout behind us.

'Here comes Bull,' I said, relieved.

'A bull?' He was blinking nervously.

'Don't worry.' I patted him kindly on the arm. 'He doesn't charge at people. He's just so big and strong that the earth shakes when he walks. He's reasonably gentle once you get to know him. Just doesn't know his own strength.'

Simpson didn't look reassured.

'Thanks, Ali. I . . . er . . . is it all right if I tag along with you? I don't know where the range is exactly, or how to do the drills.'

Bull had joined us. He stared at Simpson.

'Who's this?'

'Simpson,' I said. 'He's new.'

We walked along together.

'Have you heard about Carson?' Bull asked me.

My heart missed a beat as it always did at the mention of Carson's name.

'What about him?' I said.

'He's joined the corps. He's taking up shooting. He wants to get into the Shooting Eleven.'

Bull's voice was neutral. I was biting my lips.

'I thought he was too busy being captain of football,' I said.

'He's injured his knee. Can't play for the rest of the term. And he's aiming for Sandhurst and the army so he's keen to win a cup or two.'

I said nothing.

'Who's Carson?' said Simpson, shooting a timid glance at Bull, who towered over him.

'A fellow in the Sixth,' I said. 'Very popular.'

We walked on in silence.

'I wish he'd keep out of the Corps!' Bull burst out suddenly.

I looked at him, surprised. 'Why? Don't you like him?'

'I fagged for him all last term.'

'Did he beat you? Is he a bully?' asked Simpson anxiously.

'He doesn't beat much. It's not that.'

I took a deep breath and decided to risk saying what I thought for once. 'Carson's clever at being nasty,' I told Simpson. 'He digs at people. He knows how to make you feel bad. He picks someone out, then humiliates him.

Most people don't seem to notice. I'd keep out of his way if I were you.'

It was Bull's turn to look surprised. 'I thought he liked you, Ali. He takes a lot of notice of you, anyway.'

There was a tuft of grass on the path in front of me. I kicked at it viciously. I had understood for the first time how much I hated Carson.

'Not the kind of notice I'd choose,' I said.

'Good man,' said Bull enthusiastically. 'At last. Someone else who isn't fooled.'

Then he clapped me on the back so hard that I nearly toppled over. He reached out an arm and pulled me up just in time.

'Sorry, old fellow. Got a bit carried away there.'

'Beetle knows,' I said. 'He isn't fooled either.'

'Beetle?' Bull raised his eyebrows, as most people did when they thought about Beetle.

'You'd be surprised,' I said. I was used to defending Beetle. 'There's a lot more to him than people think.'

'Who's this coming along behind us?' said Simpson, looking round. 'Someone else for drill practice?'

Bull and I turned round and groaned. 'Carson,' we said, in exactly the same tone of disgust. It made us burst out laughing.

'Come on,' I said. 'I'll race you both to the butts.'

The school holidays came along soon after I'd joined the volunteer corps. I dread the holidays. If no one can be found to take me, I have to stay here at school. It's as dreary as can be. The buildings are so quiet and empty that a single person crossing the quad is an event. There's no mass of boys rushing up and down the stairs or crowding into the dining room.

The worst time is just before the end of term, when the fellows are packing to go home. They call out to each other in excitement. I have no choice but to stand by and listen.

'My father's bought a new hunter. We're taking him out with the hounds next week.'

'Treacle pudding! I can't wait. Our cook's the best at making it.'

'Be sorry for me, fellows. My sister's getting married. I've got to kiss hundreds of aunts.'

Someone always says, 'What are you doing, Alamayu?'

There's a general hush. They hope I'm going to say that I've been invited to visit the Queen.

'Oh, Scotland again,' I say airily. Or London. Or Gloucester. Or wherever it is that Chancellor Lowe has decided to send me.

It was Scotland last time, to stay with Sir Thomas and Lady Biddulph. I suppose the Queen told them to invite me, but they don't make me feel as if I'm a burden. Their son is called Victor. He's the same age as me. We don't mind each other, though we're not exactly close friends.

I quite like it when I'm at the Biddulphs'. They live in a big house in a quiet, remote place, surrounded by green hills. It's not far from Balmoral, where the Queen stays in the summer. I like to go out with the gamekeepers and stalk the deer. You can hear nothing up there on the high ground except for the larks and the bleating of sheep, the ripple of a stream and the wind ruffling the reeds. Sometimes I can almost imagine that I'm in Abyssinia, if I can ignore the rain.

Sir Thomas or Lady Biddulph takes me over to Balmoral to see the Queen. She looks the same as she does on the Isle of Wight. She wears the same clothes, sits in the same kind of room, and her daughters work away at their sewing. Just

Balmoral Castle

like at Osborne there are pictures everywhere of her dead husband, Prince Albert.

The trouble with going to Scotland is the journey. The first stretch is usually fine, because there's always someone from school on the same train as me – a master, or some boys on their way to their homes in the north. Someone meets me in Edinburgh and puts me on a train for the last leg of the journey. That's the worst part. More often than not, I travel alone, and I have to endure the stares and comments of ignorant people who have never seen a person from Africa before.

Last time it was horrible. A woman with two young girls burst into my carriage, filling it up with their huge skirts and capes and hatboxes. They stared at me rudely. Then the woman called for the guard.

'Kindly remove this person,' she said, in a high, shrill voice. She didn't even look at me. 'How did anyone let him into a first-class carriage?'

The guard was a friend of mine. I'd travelled with him before. In any case, I'd been put into his care in Edinburgh by the station master himself. He knew I would be staying close to Balmoral. He knew I was known to the Queen.

'And what would you wish me to do with him, ma'am?' he said, winking at me.

The woman had long yellow sausage ringlets hanging out from either side of her bonnet, exactly like the two girls did. She was fanning her face, which was red with anger.

'Decent people – young girls – should not be expected to travel with . . . savages,' she spat out.

I stood up and reached for my hat, which I'd put on the rack above me.

'You'd better find me another seat, Mr Wilson,' I mumbled to the guard.

He took my hat gently from my hands and replaced it on the rack.

'Not at all, Your Highness. It's the lady who'll be moving. Come along, please, madam. This compartment was reserved especially for the Prince. I hope he'll forgive you for disturbing him.'

I would have laughed at the expression on her face, the bewilderment and embarrassment, if it had been the only time such a thing had happened, but it wasn't. Something like that spoils every journey. It would have been pleasant too if there had been a friendly person in the carriage, and we could have talked to pass the time on the long journey, but I spent it alone, staring out of the window at the fine rain which swept in grey curtains across the sky.

Once I'd settled on a career in the army, I set my heart on a cavalry regiment. Whenever I've visited the Queen, at Osborne or Balmoral, I've always looked out to see if any dragoons or lancers are there. I love to see them on manoeuvres, riding in formation, wheeling and trotting, the horses shaking their bridles as they recognize the trumpet calls and move from a canter to a full charge, their riders leaning forward with their lances lowered. Father's cavalry were his elite troops. A king in Abyssinia must be able to ride, and ride well, at the head of his army.

It was Carson who shattered that dream. It happened at the beginning of term.

The volunteer corps had been out on the shooting range, and I knew I'd done well. Captain Murray came up to congratulate me.

'You have the makings of an excellent rifleman,' he said. 'Perhaps even an officer before you leave school. Keep up your attendance at the drill, Alamayu, and practise regularly. I can see a promotion to corporal any day now.'

Captain Murray is the commander-in-chief of our school corps. He's a proper schoolmaster, but an army man as well. I've always liked him, perhaps because he's never taught me a school subject. Most of the masters here raise their eyebrows and sigh whenever they deal with me. It's my fault, I suppose, for coming bottom in almost every class. But Captain Murray is different.

It was bad luck for me that Carson was standing by. He came into the corps as a private, as everyone has to, but he assumed (and the rest of us did too) that he would quickly be promoted. It's Captain Murray who promotes privates to be corporals or sergeants, but the corporals and sergeants vote to make one of their number a lieutenant, and eventually a captain. Becoming a corporal is the first step up, and Carson was desperate to take it as fast as he could.

'A word, sir, if I may,' he said, looking significantly at me.

Captain Murray took the hint. 'Run along, Alamayu. Take that rifle off Simpson. He's a danger to himself and everyone else.'

I walked away, filled with misgiving, and my suspicions were correct, because when I looked over my shoulder I could see that Captain Murray was looking at me thoughtfully as he listened to the poisonous words that Carson was dripping into his ears. I saw him question Carson closely, then slap his swagger stick against his thigh, as if he was displeased, before nodding curtly and dismissing Carson with a frown.

Carson lost no time. He sauntered up to me. 'Sorry, old fellow, I had to do it.'

'Do what, Carson?'

'I had to put the CO right on a rather difficult point. I know you'll understand. I'm afraid you won't be making it to corporal, after all. I explained to him that he can't expect white men to obey the commands of a . . . a . . .'

I recoiled from him as if he had struck me.

'A native savage darkie black,' I spat out furiously, but

immediately I felt as if I had hit myself. I had let my guard fatally slip and shown my weakness.

His eyes widened in triumph. At last he had goaded me into showing how much I hated him.

'Not my words, I assure you,' he said smoothly. 'But, well, I'm sure you'll see how it is when you've had time to think it over.'

Once I had started I couldn't pull back.

'I understand exactly, Carson, that you're a cad. A . . . a . . .'

He pushed out his lips. 'I'd be careful if I were you, *Prince*.' This time it was his mask that had slipped. He snapped his fingers in my face. 'I can make your life miserable here.'

I had myself under control again.

'You're not as powerful as you think you are,' I managed to say. 'I'm not the only person who's seen through you. You'd be quite surprised if you knew what people really think.'

I turned away, shaking with anger and hurt, but not before I'd had the satisfaction of seeing a flicker of anxiety cross his face.

I hadn't noticed Bull while Carson was talking to Captain Murray, but he must have been standing close to them because he overheard enough to come charging up to me as soon as drill practice was over.

'It's outrageous!' he stormed. 'Carson's a complete . . . a

monstrous . . . He wants to be corporal himself – that's all there is to it.'

But I had had time to calm down and think during the drill practice. My anger had turned to misery.

'Perhaps he's right,' I said. 'Maybe no one would want me to be corporal. Black men don't give orders to white men in this country. They wouldn't be accepted.'

'That's what Carson *wants* you to think!' Bull stamped furiously on the ground. 'Anyway, they wouldn't be taking orders from "a black man", but from you, Alamayu. A prince. Their comrade.'

'Thank you, Bull.'

His words had cheered me, at least for the moment. He must have spoken to some of the others too, because that evening, as I walked through the quad, I saw that someone had chalked up on the wall the words 'Alamayu for Corporal! Support the Soldier's Friend!'

It made no difference of course. Carson got his wish, and a corporal's pair of stripes decorated his arm at our next drill practice. He would exchange them soon for a sergeant's three stripes, I knew, and then would confidently expect to be voted up to lieutenant at the first opportunity.

What he hadn't bargained for, and what surprised me, was that the story of how he had denied my promotion and taken it for himself began to be whispered round the school. The fellows didn't like it. Carson was still popular, and a word of praise from him still counted, especially on the football field, but the glow that had surrounded him had begun, very slightly, to fade.

Carson was an excellent shot. His military father had taught him, I suppose. He needed only a few practice sessions to become familiar with our Snider rifles. He started angling at once to be chosen for the Eleven, the team that represents the school in shooting matches.

I was so angry after he spoiled my chances of promotion that I nearly stayed away from the next meeting of the corps. In fact, I was on the point of resigning altogether.

What's the point in carrying on? I asked myself miserably. They'll never let me get on. They'll never choose me for the First Eleven. I might as well give up now.

I decided to get out of the way of all of the other volunteers and go bug-hunting with Beetle instead.

Bull caught me as I was pulling on my boots. 'What are you doing? We'll be late for practice. Where's your uniform?'

'I'm not coming. Can't see the point.'

Bull stuck out his chin, making him look even more ferocious than usual. 'You can't back away now. Carson'll think he's won. You're as good a shot as he is. You've got to face him down. Anyway –' he looked round – 'where's that shrimp Simpson gone? Oh, there he is. Come here, Simpson. This idiot says he's not coming to practice. Tell him.'

Simpson swallowed nervously. 'I . . . please come, Ali.'

Bull laughed. 'Look at him — scared of everyone except you. Thinks you're going to look after him.'

Simpson's face flamed red. 'I'm not scared. I don't need looking after! It's just that . . .'

Beetle had appeared, his bug-collecting paraphernalia clanking as he walked. He nodded in his abrupt way. 'Bull's right, Ali. You should go.'

I hesitated. Their warmth encouraged me. Perhaps there was hope for me in the corps after all. I gave in and shrugged into my uniform coat.

'Fine friends you are,' I grumbled. 'You know you're sending me off to be insulted again.'

'Sounds like you did a nice bit of insulting yourself,' grinned Beetle. 'Wish I'd been there to see Carson's face.'

Captain Murray was embarrassed when he saw me coming.

'Ah, yes, Alamayu,' he said, not meeting my eye. 'Good. Good. Get down to the range quickly now. Sergeant Major Boucher's waiting to start instructing.'

Carson was already at the butts. My stomach tightened when I saw him. He was looking down at the rifle he was holding. Sergeant Major Boucher was bending over it, showing him how to adjust the sights. He looked up and saw us.

'Come along, boys, come along, nearly late again. I'll have you on bread and water for a week next time.'

I took a deep breath and felt better. I liked Sergeant Major Boucher. We all did. He was a proper old soldier. He had carried his gun into the slaughter at Balaclava when he was no older than us, and had come out of it with a sabre slash across his face. The scar still puckered the side of his mouth. He liked to scowl at us and threaten dreadful punishments, but he was too soft-hearted ever to carry them out.

He turned his attention back to the rifle Carson was holding.

'You just gives her a little twist with your screwdriver. Gets the alignment right, see? Hold it up to your eye, Corporal Carson, sir. That's right. Squint along the barrel. She'll fire true now. A little twist of the screw too far, or not quite far enough, and she'll aim off.'

Bull, Simpson and I walked across to the line of straw bales that had been set up, behind which we would stand to fire at the targets at the far end of the range. Captain Murray walked towards us, looking down at a list in his hand.

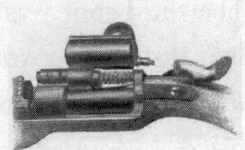

The mechanism of the Snider rifle

'As you know, all of you, the Cheltenham match is fast approaching and the moment has come to select the team of eleven who will take part. I propose to do so this afternoon.' He raised his voice. 'Sergeant Major Boucher, kindly position the rifles ready on the bales.'

The sergeant major unloaded five rifles from the cart by the side of the range and laid them at precisely equal distances along the straw bales. I measured the distance with my eyes to the targets at the far end of the field. It didn't look too far. I knew I could do well.

'Now, Sergeant Major,' Captain Murray was speaking again, 'the ammunition, if you please.'

The shoot-off for the election to the Eleven was a complicated business. There were around forty of us hopefuls. We were made to shoot in groups of five. We had to fire from three positions. The first was the easiest. We lay down on the ground, resting the barrel of the rifle on the row of straw bales. In the second round, we had to kneel, dig the stock of the gun into our left knee to anchor it, raise our right shoulders, and fire from that position. The third shot was taken standing up. It's hard to shoot like that. When you look through the sights and down the barrel, the muzzle seems to wobble about all over the place.

Captain Murray made us all line up once the rifles were laid out ready on the straw bales and the targets had been set up at the far end of the range. He always made us do things in an orderly, military way. I liked that. Father would have liked it too.

Carson was in the third group of five, and I, along with

Bull and Simpson, was in the fourth. I was looking for signs of tension in Carson, hoping that nerves would make him shoot wide. I longed for him to be humiliated in front of everyone, but there wasn't much chance of it. He was behaving with his usual confidence, talking and laughing easily to the boys in front of and behind him.

And he did shoot well. I have to admit that. Captain Murray, who didn't seem to like Carson very much, grunted with approval, and Sergeant Major Boucher called out, 'Very good shooting, Corporal Carson!'

When they'd taken their shots and the targets had been examined, Carson and the others laid the rifles back down on the straw bales ready for my group to take our places. Carson looked over his shoulder, and I could see him calculating. He saw that I would be shooting with the same rifle he had used. He hesitated for a moment, and then, instead of stepping away from the straw bales as the others had done, he bent down as if he was looking for something. He had his back to me, so that I couldn't see exactly what he was doing.

'Hurry up, Carson!' barked Captain Murray. 'We haven't got all day.'

'Sorry, sir,' said Carson, smiling confidently at Captain Murray. As he straightened up I saw him slip something into his pocket. 'I dropped this.' He removed his hand from his pocket and held up a sovereign, then stepped back so that I could take his place.

'Good luck, Alamayu,' he said loudly, so that everyone could hear. 'I'm sure you'll do very well.'

I lay down behind the bales, and lifted the rifle to look down the sights. I wanted badly to shoot well. I wanted to show Carson and everyone else how good I was. I wanted to get into the Eleven.

I heard Charlie's voice in my head.

When there's a difficult job to do, take your time. Breathe easily, Alamayu. Relax.

I took my first shot. It was a good one, I knew.

'Second position!' called out Sergeant Major Boucher.

The five of us rose to a kneeling position, carefully settled our rifles against our knees and took aim.

'In your own time, fire!'

I fired my second shot. I was feeling in control. I knew I was shooting well, but the hardest round was still to come.

'Third position,' came the command. We got to our feet and took aim. 'Steady, lads. When you're ready, fire!'

Our shots rang out across the field.

'Leave your rifles on the bales,' called out Captain Murray. 'Turn to the left and walk off.'

He walked down the range to examine the targets. As he came back, he called out, 'Well done, Simpson and Jones. Not bad for a first try, Simpson. A bit off to the left, Bulliver. Disappointing, Alamayu. You missed the target altogether.'

I stared at him, shocked and dismayed.

'Missed the target, sir? But . . .'

Someone beside me was breathing heavily. It was Bull. His face was scarlet with rage. 'Sir,' he burst out, 'it's all wrong. Carson . . . Take a look at Ali's rifle, sir, please.'

Captain Murray glared at him. 'Be quiet, boy. We can't all shoot well all the time. It's a pity, but there it is. Stand back. Let the next lot take their turn.'

'But, sir—' insisted Bull.

'That's enough, Bulliver!'

Bull clenched his fists and began to march across to where Carson was in the middle of a circle of admiring boys.

'What are you doing?' I said, catching his arm.

'Carson fiddled with the sights of your rifle. I saw him. He turned the screw with his penknife to make you shoot wide.'

'He can't have done! How could he? He didn't have time.'

He shook me off. I held on to him.

'Only takes a minute. You saw him, pretending to drop something. Let me *go*, Ali.'

Even I couldn't believe that Carson had been capable of such a trick. I didn't see how he could have taken such a risk.

'He'll deny it. You can't prove it anyway. I shot badly. I must have done.'

The next group of boys was already in their first position. Their first volley rang out.

I was thinking rapidly.

'Look,' I said. 'It's Pettifer on my rifle. He's one of the best in the corps. Let's see if he shoots wide. Then we'll know.'

Captain Murray shook his head as he walked back from examining the targets.

'What's the matter with you, Pettifer? Right off to the left. Worst I've ever seen you shoot.'

'Sir!' yelled Bull, unable to contain himself any longer. 'Examine Pettifer's rifle, Captain Murray, sir. It's been tampered with!'

I don't think that Captain Murray would have done anything about the faulty rifle if he had had his way. He was a straightforward sort of military man. He couldn't imagine that anyone would stoop so low as to cheat in a shooting contest. He was more concerned with suppressing Bull's undisciplined outburst.

I stood unnoticed by everyone, almost unable to take in what was happening, twisting my hands together in a kind of excited dread.

Sergeant Major Boucher hadn't liked the suggestion that one of his precious rifles wasn't firing straight after he had personally adjusted the sights. He had picked up the rifle that Carson, Pettifer and I had shot with and examined it closely.

'I've had enough from you, Bulliver,' Captain Murray was saying. 'I won't stand for indiscipline in the ranks. One more word out of you, and—'

'Captain Murray, sir, I think you ought to take a look at this,' Sergeant Major Boucher interrupted unhappily.

'What? What is it?' Captain Murray turned impatiently.

The sergeant major laid the rifle in his hands.

'The sights, sir. Twisted out of true. But I adjusted them myself, sir. I know they was good when the young gentlemen started firing.'

Captain Murray held the rifle close to his eyes and closely examined the sights. 'How did this happen, Boucher? Could the screw have worked loose?'

'No, sir. Look at it yourself. There's scratch marks on it. It wasn't a proper screwdriver that made those, sir, but a penknife or suchlike. This gun was in perfect order when Mr Carson was shooting with it.'

'Captain Murray!' burst out Bull. 'I'm trying to tell you! I saw him – Carson! I saw him twist the screw with a penknife!'

My palms were slippery with sweat. I found I was holding my breath. The whole corps had crowded round. The boys were watching and listening avidly. Carson, in front of the mob, spread out his hands, putting his head on one side and smiling in his charming way.

'Sir, surely, you can't think that . . .'

The other boys were edging away from him.

Captain Murray stared at him, frowning. 'I find it impossible to believe that any decent boy, any *Rugby* boy, would stoop so low as to cheat.'

'Of *course* I haven't cheated, sir! It's a despicable suggestion.' Carson took a step forward. I thought for a moment that he was going to lay a confiding hand on Captain Murray's arm, but the captain was glaring at him so coldly that Carson halted.

'I . . . I'm afraid that the sergeant major, excellent man though he is, must have slipped up, sir. He can't have tightened the screw properly. Accidents happen all the time, don't they, sir?'

Everyone's head swivelled across to look at the sergeant major, who was showing signs of distress, his face a dull red.

'Not fair, to blame poor old Boucher,' the boy next to me muttered.

'*Sir!*' Bull cried out desperately.

Captain Murray hesitated for a moment longer, then he said, 'Turn out your pockets, Carson.'

Carson was still smiling, but his smile was slowly freezing on his face. My heart was thudding, the blood singing in my ears.

'Really, sir, this is ridiculous! A wild accusation by a jealous younger boy . . .'

'Your pockets.'

Shrugging his shoulders, and casting a scornful glance around the ring of watching faces, Carson pulled both his jacket pockets fully out and held up in triumph one handkerchief and one gold sovereign.

The watching boys let out an 'Oh!' of relief, but I gripped my hands together in disappointment.

It was Simpson who saved the day. He had darted across to the straw bale from which I had been shooting and was hunting round on the ground.

'Please, sir, I've found something,' he squeaked, holding up a penknife.

Carson took a step backwards. 'That's not mine, Captain,' he said breathlessly. 'On the word of a . . . a Rugbeian.'

'Give that thing to me, Simpson,' barked Captain Murray.

A new hope was surging inside me. Simpson, blushing hotly under the gaze of so many fascinated eyes, took the penknife across to Captain Murray and dropped it into his hand. Captain Murray turned it over.

'What's your full name, Carson?'

'Stephen Richard Carson!' called out one of Carson's friends. He had been watching Carson at first with shock and now with horror, and was standing with his arms crossed, his shoulders hunched in disgust.

'Not yours, Carson?' said Captain Murray. 'Then why are the initials SRC engraved on this penknife?'

There was a long pause. Carson looked round wildly at the circle of boys who were shuffling their feet, looking anywhere but at him, refusing to meet his eyes.

'Look here, fellows, you don't believe this nonsense, do you? Why would I mess things up for Alamayu? You all know what a friend I've been to him.'

I could stand in silence no longer.

'My friend? You?' I burst out. 'You've humiliated me in every way you can. I wasn't the one to accuse you of cheating, but what you've done doesn't surprise me. It's the kind of person you are.'

A snarl of rage and loathing contorted Carson's face. 'You snivelling little black slave,' he hissed. 'I'll . . .'

He lunged towards me, his fists balled. I made myself stand still and face him. I wasn't going to let him see me flinch. At the last minute he stopped himself, dropped his fists and took a deep breath. He was biting his lip so hard that I thought it would bleed.

'Carson,' said Captain Murray in a grating voice, 'you are stripped of your rank of corporal and banned from the Corps. You will come with me now to the Headmaster. Carry on please, Sergeant Major.'

There was an atmosphere of stunned disbelief as the figures of Captain Murray and Carson disappeared in the direction of School House.

'Carson, of all people!' one of Carson's sixth-form friends said. 'I mean – Carson!'

'He's been so keen on, well, on morality,' said another. 'You know, quoting the scriptures, and giving guidance to the younger boys.'

'Preaching and prating, you mean,' muttered Bull.

'Hey, Alamayu!' Another sixth-former beckoned me

over. 'It's not true, what you said about Carson to old
Murray, is it? About him humiliating you? What did you
mean by it?'

The group of older boys was large, pressing around me.
They were all taller than me. I had fagged for one or two
of them. I breathed in deeply, but my voice still came out
in an embarrassing squeak.

'Carson thinks,' I said, choosing my words carefully,
'that people from . . . from other races . . . are inferior.
He thinks I – we – should be kept in our place. He enjoys
pointing this out to me. He does it cleverly, pretending to
be kind.'

There, I said to myself. I've said it now.

I saw two of Carson's friends exchange glances, then
look away from me.

'A bit oversensitive, aren't you?' said one.

Before I had a chance to answer, there was a snort behind
me. 'Ali's not being oversensitive,' Bull said, planting his
heavy feet squarely beside me. 'Carson's a hypocrite. He's
a liar. He chipped Jardine's cricket bat last summer and
blamed Stephens for it. Gave him a talking-to for hours
about looking after other people's property. Stephens
tried to tell the other fellows, but no one believed him.
I did, though. Look how Carson tried to drop poor old
Boucher in it.'

'He takes things off us,' another boy piped up. 'My cake.'

Over by the straw bales, Sergeant Major Boucher had

been readjusting the rifle, shaking his head with shocked disapproval as he did so.

'Right, boys. You heard Captain Murray,' he called out suddenly. 'Carry on, that's what we've got to do. Can't stand around here all day. Pettifer and Alamayu, you'll take your shots again. Stand back, the rest of you. Let these two show us what they're made of.'

Hands patted me on the back as I got ready for my second try at the target.

'Good luck, Ali,' several boys called out. 'You show 'em!'

My hands trembled as I picked up the rifle and prepared to shoot. Sergeant Major Boucher was standing above me.

'Take your time, Mr Alamayu, sir.' His voice was slow and steady. 'A deep breath in. That's right. Hold the rifle still. We don't want it bobbing about like a fart in a thunderstorm, now, do we?'

Everyone burst out laughing. The tension eased. I could focus now. I could hold the rifle still. I took in my breath, held it, let it out and pulled the trigger.

'Second position!' barked Sergeant Major Boucher, reverting to his authoritarian manner.

I was in control now. I took my second shot, and then the third.

'Stand aside,' the

The Snider rifle

sergeant major said. 'Mr Bulliver, kindly check the target.'

Bull took off and sprinted down the range.

'Two right through the centre, Sergeant Major,' he called back gleefully, 'and the third an inch to the right!'

'Do you think I'll get into the Eleven, Sergeant Major?' Pettifer asked eagerly, after he had fired his three shots.

'I wouldn't rightly know what Captain Murray will say when he's had a chance to look at the targets,' answered Sergeant Major Boucher, but as he turned away from Pettifer he saw me looking at him, winked, and laid a finger along the side of his nose.

I didn't have time to enjoy the surge of excitement that rushed through me. A figure had appeared in the distance, its arms wildly waving round its head.

'Beetle!' said Bull. 'What does he want? He never comes near the range.'

Beetle ran up panting, the specimen jars dangling from his neck on their strings, swinging wildly.

'Ran into Captain Murray,' he panted. 'Says that Ali, Bull, Simpson and Pettifer have to go at once to the headmaster. And Mr Boucher too. He looked furious. What's going on?'

My spirits, which had just risen so high, sank again.

'Carson's talked his way out of it – you mark my words,' groaned Bull.

'Yes, he's in there blaming it all on us,' said Pettifer.

Sergeant Major Boucher seemed suddenly to inflate.

He looked like a bullfrog that had blown himself up to bursting point.

'Lyin's one thing, and cheatin's another,' he bellowed. 'But sabotagin' army property is what I won't stand for. Downright dangerous it is. Downright immoral. You come with me, lads. We'll put the headmaster right.'

'But what's going on?' pleaded Beetle.

'Tell you later,' I said, and sprinted after the others.

It was obvious as soon as we filed into Dr Jex-Blake's study that Bull had been right. If Carson hadn't quite talked his way out of trouble, it looked as if he was well on the way to it. He was sitting comfortably on a chair in front of the headmaster's desk, at his ease. Something he had just said had made Dr Jex-Blake smile, a smile that faded when he looked up to see us file into the room. Captain Murray was standing by the door, his arms folded across his chest, a thunderous frown on his face.

'Now then,' said Dr Jex-Blake heavily. 'A very serious accusation has been made against Carson, which, in the light of his moral standing in the school and his excellent character, I find hard to believe. There appears to be malice on the part of some –' he glared at Bull, Simpson and me – 'and, let us say, inefficiency on the part of others.'

His eyes flickered over the sergeant major as he said this, and old Boucher stiffened till he looked like a fence post, and with a wooden face fixed his eyes on a point above Dr Jex-Blake's head.

'Explain the matter to me, if you please,' Dr Jex-Blake went on. 'You begin, Alamayu.'

I don't think I was a very good witness. In fact, I can't remember what I said as I stumbled through the story. The blood was hammering so loudly in my ears that I couldn't think clearly. Carson's look of patient sorrow was almost more than I could bear, but as we spoke – Bull, Pettifer, Simpson and me – one after the other, I saw that Carson's knuckles were white and that sweat was breaking out on his forehead.

Sergeant Major Boucher brought himself to attention when it was his turn to speak.

'I have been accused of dereliction of duty,' he said stiffly, 'of lack of care of army property. That being the case, I resign my position with the corps.'

'Don't be foolish, man.' Captain Murray, who had been listening closely, watching one of us after the other, peeled himself off the wall against which he had been leaning and advanced across the room towards the headmaster's desk.

'These boys are telling the truth, Headmaster,' he said. 'Corporal Carson is guilty of gross deception and sabotage. He was motivated not only by ambition to shoot for the school but by personal animosity towards Private Alamayu.'

Dr Jex-Blake looked flustered. 'Need we bother with military rank?' he said irritably. 'This is hardly a court martial. I'm sure we can get to the bottom of it without . . .'

Carson cleared his throat. 'If I may speak, sir. It's nonsense to say that I don't like Alamayu. Ask anyone in the school! I have befriended him, taken notice of him, done everything I could to—'

'To deny him promotion in the corps!' interrupted Captain Murray. 'Headmaster, Carson told me, when he learned that I was considering Alamayu for promotion, that he thought the other boys in the corps would refuse to serve under a black man. I should have looked into the matter further, but I'm afraid that I took his word for it, reluctant though I was.'

Dr Jex-Blake's eyebrows twitched together.

'Is this true, Carson?'

Carson licked his lips. 'It's true that I – that in my – in an *honest* opinion, sir . . .'

A fly which had been buzzing round the room chose that moment to land on my cheek. I suppose my cheek twitched. I suppose it must have looked as if I was smiling. It was sheer luck that Carson thought so. It flicked him on the raw.

'You can wipe that smile off your face!' he burst out, his charm dropping away from him like a falling cloak. 'They should never have let a savage like you into the company of decent white men!'

I don't think it was his words that condemned him in the eyes of Dr Jex-Blake. It was the hatred ringing in his voice and the startling change in his manner. Carson, aware of the stillness that had fallen on the room, swivelled round in sudden anxiety to find the headmaster staring coldly at him from under heavy brows.

'You are a grave disappointment to me, Carson, and a disgrace to Rugby School. I have never been so deceived by a boy in my life. I shall write to your father this evening and ask him to remove you tomorrow.'

Carson had gone pale. He started up from his chair. 'Sir, please! They've all been lying to you! Sir!'

'Out!' barked Captain Murray. 'Now.'

I was in a hurry to leave myself, but the headmaster hadn't finished with me.

'Alamayu,' he said, his face puzzled, 'I am, as you know, in the position of a parent to you. If you have been teased or bullied because of your appearance, you ought to have come to me. Is there anything else you wish to tell me?'

I felt my face grow hot. I knew that he had never felt much affection for me, and I had felt none for him.

'There's nothing, sir. Thank you, sir.'

'Very well. But don't hesitate, if . . .'

'No, sir. Of course not, sir.'

Captain Murray coughed and looked meaningfully at Sergeant Major Boucher, who was still standing motionless, staring stonily straight ahead.

'Ah yes,' sighed Dr Jex-Blake. 'Sergeant Major. You have clearly been falsely accused. I am assured by Captain Murray that you have always carried out your duties to the highest possible standard. I beg you to reconsider your offer to resign.'

Sergeant Major Boucher visibly relaxed. 'I will, sir. Thank you very much.'

Beetle was hovering outside the Headmaster's study when at last I emerged. He grabbed my arm.

'*Now* will you tell me what's going on? Carson just came out of there as white as a sheet. Ali, what are you jumping about like that for? Bull, put Ali down! Why are you all laughing? For goodness sake, someone *tell* me!'

I like savouring the moment of Carson's downfall. It makes me smile to think of how he was expelled, even as I lie here. His expulsion caused such a scandal in Rugby School that for days no one could think of anything else. I was suddenly the centre of everyone's attention. Boys kept asking me questions like, 'Is it true that Carson tortured you in secret?' and 'Did Carson really steal Simpson's watch?' and 'Have you told the Queen about Carson?'

I answered as best I could but I always felt uncomfortable.

Bull was thrilled by what happened. 'Just goes to show,' he said later, kicking out at a clod of earth and making it shoot up into the air, 'that there is justice in this world.

A fellow can't be as rotten as Carson without everyone finding out eventually, even if he is good at making himself popular.'

Beetle shook his head. 'Carson's still popular. To some,' he said.

Bull lurched round in front of me and pushed his face right into Beetle's. 'What do you mean? We won, didn't we?'

'No,' said Beetle. He pushed Bull away and walked off towards the stream, and though Bull kept calling after him, he wouldn't turn round and answer.

I kept thinking about what Beetle had said, and later, in the evening, went to find him in his study.

'You've heard things,' I said straight out. 'What are people saying?'

'What about?' said Beetle.

He was working away at a stick with his penknife, as he often did.

'You hear more than others do,' I persisted. 'People think you're not listening, because you don't say much, so they talk out in front of you.'

'What if they do?'

'Come on, Beetle!' I was starting to feel impatient. 'I really want to know.'

He picked up another stick and started whittling pieces off the end of it. 'All right then. I've heard a few fellows say that it wasn't fair, Carson being expelled.'

I felt the blood rush to my head. 'Not fair? After what happened?'

He shot a look at me. 'You wanted me to tell you. They liked him too much. They can't believe he did what he did.'

'I suppose they think I pulled a trick. To get him into trouble,' I said furiously.

I hadn't meant it, and was shocked when Beetle nodded.

'So I suppose they think Carson was right when he stopped me being a corporal. That . . . that black fellows can't give orders to white ones.'

'Something like that,' Beetle said unwillingly.

'Well then. *Well* then.' I felt as if I'd been punched in the stomach. 'That's *my* future gone up in smoke. It doesn't exactly sound as if I've got prospects in the British Army, does it?'

Beetle's knife slipped, nicking his hand.

'Ouch!' he said sharply, putting his bleeding finger up to his mouth and sucking it.

'Before you came to Rugby everyone thought the way Carson thinks,' he said in a muffled voice. ''Spose I did. No one knew anyone like you.'

I wrenched my handkerchief out of my pocket and gave it to him.

'You'd better wrap this round your hand before you get blood everywhere.'

'Point is, Ali,' he said, bandaging up his finger, 'it's as I said. Not everyone thinks like Carson. Not any more. Lots of fellows don't. Because they know you.'

The school clock chimed.

'Supper,' he said with relief, making for the door.

I felt low as Beetle and I joined the stream of boys following the smell of boiled beef and carrots. I didn't feel like eating. As long as I stayed in Britain there would be other Carsons to torment me. I knew that I would never be free of them.

Someone jostled me, pushing me against the wall as he rushed past. I felt a burst of anger.

I'm a prince! I told myself. No one cares about that here.

I can still feel that kick of anger, and I suppose it will always be with me, but I've had time to think about what Beetle said too. He was right. I have changed people's opinions here in Rugby. No one calls me 'darkie' or 'blackie' any more. Perhaps I could make a difference in the wider world as well. In spite of everything, I might one day be accepted in the army. After all, I was picked for the Shooting Eleven. And Captain Murray has sent me a note, here in the sickroom, telling me that as soon as I return to the corps I'll be promoted to corporal.

I think I'm getting better. I hope I am. The fever was down last night, but now I feel so weak that I can hardly lift my hand. Is this how Amma felt when they were carrying her down the mountainside in her dooley?

I don't know what it was that killed Amma. 'Pleurisy,' Charlie said once, 'but probably consumption.'

Consumption's a terrible disease. People usually die of it. It can't be what's wrong with me. I won't believe it.

I'm sure I've just had a touch of pneumonia. It was my fault too, in a way. And the fault of the lion.

It started when Beetle and I walked into Rugby town two weeks ago. I've never liked going into town on my own because of the way people stare at me. It's better than it was when I first came, because the townsfolk are used to seeing me now, but it's still unpleasant. Children call out, 'Hey, you! Why don't you wash the dirt off?' and 'Watch out, everyone, here comes the black monkey again!' I ignore them and don't show them how bad they make me feel. Beetle growls like an angry dog and makes little rushes at them. He swings his long arms and they run away, shrieking.

For once, no one took any notice of me. Everyone was crowding round a man who was strolling up and down holding a pole with a notice stuck on top of it.

'What is it? What's going on?' Beetle asked a stout woman with a basket on her arm.

'A travelling menagerie, my dear,' she said. 'Coming tomorrow. Elephants. Monkeys. Tigers, I shouldn't wonder.'

'You boys had better behave yourselves,' another woman chimed in. 'If you don't, they'll feed you to the lions.'

They went off together laughing.

Beetle grunted with enthusiasm. 'This is a chance to make some observations. It's a half-holiday tomorrow. Want to come with me?'

I shook my head at Beetle, but I didn't say anything. The idea of travelling animals disturbed me, I didn't know why.

The notice hadn't lied. The menagerie came. All the fellows at school went to see it. In the end I couldn't keep back my curiosity and I tagged along with them. The boys poked sticks through the bars at the lions, trying to make them roar, and threw apples to the monkeys to watch them fight over them.

I looked on for a while, but the sight of those poor creatures cowering in their cages disgusted me and I went back to school alone. Later that evening, though, after supper, I couldn't get the animals out of my mind. We're not supposed to go into town at night, but I knew I had to see them again. I slipped quietly down the stairs from my study, opened the front door of Elsee house and ran the short distance into town.

The menagerie wasn't far away. The crowds had gone and the men were packing up. They were due to move on early the next day, and they were loading animal feed on to carts and taking down the fence which had kept non-paying customers away from the cages.

It was easy for me to slip into their camp. I found myself beside a cage with a lion inside it. He was sitting on his haunches, shaking his head from side to side. In the light of a lantern hanging from a nearby post, I could see that he was staring vacantly into nothingness. I waved my hand gently, trying to get him to look at me.

'Hello,' I said.

He turned and stared at me. His eyes were empty and I

thought they looked very sad. I would have liked to reach through the bars and stroke his thick fur. I would have liked to comfort him.

'Oi!' someone shouted behind me. 'You there! Get away from that cage. We're closed!'

'Sorry,' I answered, moving back a pace.

It wasn't enough for the man. He hurried up to me. He had been forking straw into the elephant's cage and he was waving his pitchfork at me.

'You can't just come in to see the animals. You've got to pay. Missed your chance now. It's too late. I told you, we're closed.'

'It's all right, I'm going.' I moved back another step. 'Please, can I ask you something? Where did this lion come from? Is he from Africa? From Abyssinia, maybe?'

'What do I care?' The man leaned forward to peer at me. 'You ought to know, a darkie like you. You're an African yourself, by the looks of you. What does it matter where it comes from? It's a lion, that's all.'

I hated that man. I pretended to walk away, but as soon as his back was turned I crept back to the cage. The lion had risen to his feet and was standing close to the bars. He was peering out at me, as if he was waiting for me to do something. To rescue him, maybe.

I suppose it was dangerous, doing what I did, but I felt not a shred of fear. I put my hand in through the bars of the cage and stroked the lion's rough, ragged mane.

Emperor Theodore marches with his lions

'Hello, Gobezu,' I whispered. 'We're both far away from home, you and I. Did you know my father? Did you walk with him?'

He turned his head on one side, like a cat does when it wants its neck scratched. I obliged. In the distance the school clock chimed. It was a quarter to ten. I would have to run if I was to creep back into Elsee house before the doors were locked. I pulled my hand away.

'I'm sorry, Gobezu. I have to go,' I told the lion.

He made a little mewing noise, like a disappointed cat. I hesitated. My hand was still holding one of the bars. The lion turned his head and began to lick my fingers with his rough, rasping tongue. His smell took hold in my nostrils. I breathed in deeply that rich, long-forgotten mustiness of lion.

I couldn't leave him. I sank down on the straw that had fallen out of his cage and began to murmur into his ear.

I don't know what I told that lion during the long hours of darkness. I hardly heard the school clock chime each quarter hour. As the cold of that frosty night set in on me, making my teeth chatter and my limbs shiver, I felt his loneliness enter my soul.

They found me in the morning, lying against the bars of the cage. The lion was curled up on the other side, and our backs were touching. The man who had shouted at me the night before drove me away from the cage with lunges of his pitchfork.

I was feeling strange before I even reached the school. My absence had been noticed, and a storm broke over my head. I hardly heard the angry voices. This fever took hold of me and I fainted. I came round here in the sickroom, lying in this bed.

It's evening time again. The lamp has been lit and the light flickers on the ceiling overhead. The walls are not bulging forward any longer. No one is trying to break through to me and take hold of my mind.

I won't try to sit up yet. I would only faint. The fever has gone, but I'm tired to the depths of my bones.

I've been on a long, long journey.

'Who is this boy?' those voices asked me. 'What's he doing here?'

I know how to answer them now.

'I'm Prince Alamayu of Abyssinia,' I say. 'Son of the great Emperor Theodore and the noble Queen Tirunesh. I'm a schoolboy in England. I'm training to be a soldier. One day I'll return to my country as my father's heir.'

I was wrong. Not all those people have gone away. It's as if someone has heard me.

Amma is here. I shut my eyes and see the outline of her shape, the soft *shamma* draping her head and the glint of gold around her neck. She's standing above me, a little way away.

'Is that all you are, my darling?' she calls down to me. 'Is that all you can say?'

'No,' I tell her. 'I've been lonely and frightened, but I've survived. I've made friends, and I've defeated the enemy who tried to destroy me.'

This stuffy sickroom fades away, the bitter smell of medicine dissolves into cold, clear mountain air, the wooden floorboards underneath my iron bedstead have become a stony hillside. Eagles fly in the sky above me. From the cliffs below comes the call of a baboon.

Amma's face is still shrouded, but someone else stands beside her now. Father is here. He's holding Hamra by the bridle, and the horse's mane flutters in the breeze. Our warriors carrying their shields are massed behind him. My heart skips a beat. Will he frown? Will his black eyes flash with anger?

I won't be afraid of him any more. I take a deep breath and walk up the steep path towards him. He steps forward to meet me and puts a hand on my shoulder.

'You've done well, Alamayu,' he says. 'I'm proud of you, my son.'

Afterword

Prince Alamayu never did return to Abyssinia. After he left Rugby School he spent a year at Sandhurst, training to become an officer in the British Army, but he was unhappy there.

A short while after he left Sandhurst, he fell ill and died. The underlying cause of his death was probably tuberculosis, known as 'consumption' in those days, which may also have been the cause of his mother's death.

Queen Victoria was distressed when she heard the news. She wrote in her journal: 'Was grieved and shocked to hear by telegram that good Alamayu had passed away this morning. It is too sad. All alone in a strange country, without seeing a person or a relative belonging to him, so young and so good . . .'

She arranged for him to be buried among the kings and queens in the Royal Chapel at Windsor, where he still lies. There is a memorial plaque to him in the north-west corner of the nave and another in the chapel at Rugby School.

Charlie and Tiny Speedy never had children of their own. They remained devoted to the memory of Prince Alamayu throughout their long lives of service and travels in different parts of the world.

Prince Alamayu probably never read his grandmother's letter. It lay for years in a drawer at the Foreign Office, forgotten. This is what it said:

Grandmother to Grandson Alemayehu:

May this word reach Dejazmach Alemayehu,
Sent by Wayzaro Lakiyaye, mother of Itege
Tirunesh and where I am, is your mother's
country at Dejazmach Wube's church.

My child, my dear, how are you, indeed?
Ever since we parted up till today, why
did you not send me a letter?

While I die in grief and mourning, I have
no other son, no other hope but you.

Now, quickly, send me a letter, providing
your likeness in a picture so that I may
always see it.
May Christ enable us to meet! Amen.
Be friendly towards the English Queen, the
Russian King, the French King, towards all
the Kings. Send letters.

All the people of Abyssinia are awaiting
you, are desirous of you. Be wise; open the
eyes of the people of Abyssinia, for they
have become blind. Open up science for them;
let them not remain thus, blind as they
are. May God enable us to meet!

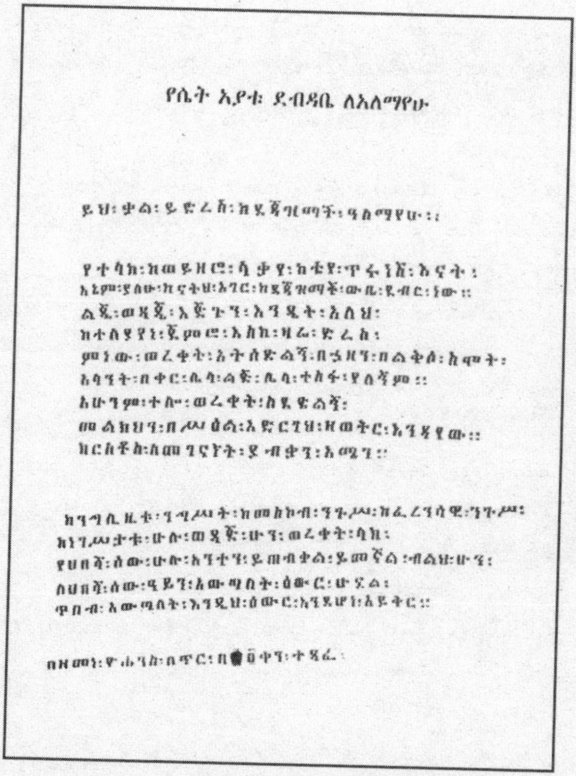

የሴት እያቴ ደብዳቤ ለአለማየሁ

ይህ፡ ቃሉ፡ ይድረ ሌ፡ ከኔ ጃግሪጣኞ፡ ዓ ለ ማየሁ፡፡

የተባክ፡ከ ወ ዩ ዘ ሮ ኔ፡ ሳ ቃ የ፡ ከ ቲ የ፡ ጥ ሩ ነ ኧ፡ እ ኛ ት ፡
ኢዶ ሙ፡ የ ለ ሙ፡ ከ ኮ ዶ ዙ፡ ኧ ገ ር፡ ኧ ጻ ጃ ዝ ሙ ሣ ኛ ፡ ሙ ሊ ፡ ዶ ብ ር ፡ ነ ሙ ፡፡
ል ጃ ፡ ወ � ጃ ፡ እ ኞ ጌ ኚ ፡ እ ኝ ዲ ት ፡ እ ለ ህ ፡
ከ ተ ለ ያ የ ፡ ጃ ጣ ሙ ፡ እ ለ ክ ፡ ሣ ረ ፡ ድ ረ ስ ፡
ሥ ነ ሙ ፡ ወ ረ ቀ ት ፡ እ ት ለ ጽ ሣ ኛ ፡ በ ጋ ዝ ፡ በ ል ቀ ለ ፡ ኧ ሙ ት ፡
ኧ ጓ ጉ ት ፡ በ ቀ ር ፡ ሊ ሳ ዕ ኝ ፡ ሊ ለ ተ ለ ቱ ፡ የ ለ ኝ ሙ ፡፡
ኧ ሁ ጉ ሙ ፡ ተ ለ ሙ ፡ ወ ረ ቀ ት ፡ ለ ዩ ድ ለ ኛ ፡
ሙ ል ክ ህ ግ ፡ በ ሣ ሳ ዕ ሰ ፡ እ ጅ ር ጉ ዝ ፡ ዝ ወ ት ቀ ር ፡ እ ጓ ጃ የ ሙ ፡፡
ክ ር ከ ቾ ክ ፡ ለ ጠ ጓ የ ት ፡ የ ብ ቋ ኑ ፡ እ ጣ ን ፡፡

ክ ጓ ግ ሊ ዚ ቱ ፡ ጉ ጣ ሣ ት ፡ ከ ወ ለ ከ ብ ፡ ጓ ጉ ሣ ፡ ኧ ፋ ረ ጓ ሳ ዊ ፡ ጓ ጉ ሙ ፡
ክ ጓ ሙ ሣ ታ ቱ ፡ ሁ ሉ ፡ ወ ጀ ኞ ፡ ሁ ጓ ፡ ወ ረ ቀ ት ፡ ሣ ክ ፡
የ ሁ በ ኞ ፡ ለ ሙ ፡ ሁ ሉ ፡ ኧ ጓ ተ ኝ ፡ ዶ መ ሣ ቀ ሰ ፡ ዶ ሙ ኛ ለ ፡ ብ ል ዝ ፡ ሁ ግ ፡
ለ ሁ በ ኝ ፡ ለ ሙ ፡ ዓ ዶ የ ፡ ኧ ሙ ሣ ስ ት ፡ ዕ ሙ ር ፡ ሁ ዶ ለ ፡
ዋ በ ብ ፡ ኧ ሙ ዋ ለ ት ፡ እ ጓ ዶ ሁ ፡ ዕ ሙ ር ፡ ኧ ጓ ዶ የ ሙ ፡ ኧ ዶ ቀ ር ፡፡

በ ዘ መ ነ ፡ ዋ ሐ ነ ከ ፡ በ ጥ ር ፡ በ ⬤ ⓪ ቀ ጓ ፡ ተ ጻ ፈ ፡

This is how the letter from Alamayu's
grandmother looked in Amharic

Acknowledgements

Many people have helped me write this book. I'm particularly grateful to Dr Sandy Holt-Wilson, who shared with me his extensive archive of material on Prince Alamayu, and lent me some of his precious books. He also gave permission for the reproduction of the drawing of Alamayu at the start of the book, and the photograph of him at the end.

At Rugby School, the archivist Rusty Maclean kindly allowed me to browse the school's archive and showed me round the fields and buildings which Alamayu must have known so well.

I would also like to thank the staff at the Victoria and Albert Museum, who showed me the clothes of Queen Tirunesh, Alamayu's mother, and, as always, the staff of the London Library.

This book is dedicated to my old friends and colleagues Michael and Patsy Sargent, who share with me a great interest in and love for Ethiopia, and who kindly read and commented on the manuscript.

Alamayu

Prince Alamayu as an English schoolboy

A
LITTLE
PIECE of
GROUND

ELIZABETH LAIRD

If you enjoyed this book, why not try
A Little Piece of Ground. Turn the page to
read the first chapter . . .

1

K arim sat on the edge of his bed, his head framed by
the mass of football posters which covered the wall.
He was frowning at the piece of paper in his hand.
The ten best things that I want to do (or be) in my life, he
had written, *by Karim Aboudi, 15 Jaffa Apartments, Ramallah,
Palestine*. Carefully, he underlined it.

Underneath, in his best handwriting, he listed:

1. *Champion footballer of the entire world (even I can dream).*
2. *Extremely cool, popular and good-looking and at least 1.90
   metres tall (or anyway taller than Jamal).*
3. *The liberator of Palestine and a national hero.*
4. *Famous TV presenter or actor (famous, anyway).*
5. *Best-ever creator of new computer games.*
6. *My own person, allowed to do what I like without parents and
   big brothers and teachers on my back all the time.*
7. *Inventor of an acid formula to dissolve reinforced steel as used
   in tanks and helicopter gunships (Israeli ones).*
8. *Stronger than Joni and my other mates (this is not asking
   much).*

He stopped and began to chew the end of his biro. In the

distance, the sound of an ambulance siren wailed through the afternoon air. He lifted his head and stared out of the window. His eyes, large and dark, peered out from under the straight black hair which framed his slim, tanned face.

He started writing again.

9. *Alive. Plus, if I have to get shot, only in places that heal up. Not in the head or spine,* inshallah.
10.

But number ten defeated him. He decided to keep the slot free in case a good idea should come to him later.

He read through what he'd written and sat for a while, tapping the end of the biro against the collar of his striped sweatshirt, then he took a fresh sheet of paper. More quickly this time, he wrote:

The ten things I don't want to do (or be)
1. *Not a shopkeeper like Baba.*
2. *Not a doctor, like Mama keeps saying I should. (Why? She knows I hate blood.)*
3. *Not short.*
4. *Not married to a girl like Farah.*
5. *Not shot in the back and stuck in a wheelchair for the rest of my life like that boy who used to go to my school.*
6. *Not spotty like Jamal.*
7. *Not having our house flattened by Israeli tanks and ending up in some lousy tent.*
8. *Not having to go to school. At all.*
9. *Not living under occupation. Not being stopped all the time by Israeli soldiers. Not being scared. Not being trapped indoors.*
10. *Not dead.*

He read his lists through again. They weren't quite right.

There were things, important things, that he'd left out, he was sure of it.

He heard raised voices outside the door. His brother, Jamal, was arguing with their mother. He would come into their shared bedroom in a minute and Karim's moment of peace would be over.

He reached down for the box under his bed, in which he kept his private things, ready to stow his lists inside it, but before he could squirrel them away, Jamal had burst into the room.

It was obvious at first glance that Jamal was in a bad mood. His brown eyes, under the wedge of black hair that fell across his forehead, snapped with irritation. Karim tried to hide his lists behind his back, but Jamal lunged forwards and whisked them out of his hands.

'What's all this secrecy about, then?' he said. 'What are you plotting, you little creep?'

Karim jumped up and tried to grab the sheets of paper back again, but Jamal, who was tall for his seventeen years, was holding them above his head, out of Karim's reach. Karim dived at his brother and pulled at the belt loop of his jeans, trying to wrestle him down onto his bed, but Jamal kept him off easily with one hand, and, still holding the lists out of reach, read through them both.

Karim waited, his face burning, for the scornful comments that he knew would come. They did.

'Champion footballer? You?' sneered Jamal. 'With your two left feet? I think I can see you scoring a goal in the World Cup – or not. You? Liberator of Palestine? With your brains – or lack of?'

Karim swallowed. There was no point in fighting with Jamal. The best thing was to pretend he didn't care.

'Don't worry,' he said, as casually as he could. 'Jealousy is a natural emotion. When I'm world-famous I'll be good to you. I won't hold anything you say against you, not even that

5

crack about my feet, which is totally unfair because I can cream a ball in between the goalposts like Zinedine Zidane any time I like.'

Jamal threw the pieces of paper back to him. He was bored with the subject already.

'So you ought to be able to,' he said, 'seeing as how you've probably spent at least a year of your life kicking that damned football against the wall downstairs, on and on and on, driving everyone in this building totally nuts.'

Cheated out of a proper fight with his little brother, he began to box the air, kicking Karim's nearly new best trainers out of the way and shuffling around in the small space between the beds as if it was a miniature boxing ring.

Karim went to the window and stared down at the ground, five storeys below. An empty plot lay next to the apartment block. It had been flattened, ready for the builders to start work, but nothing had happened there so far. Karim had made it his own, his personal football ground, the place where he played his special game.

He could feel his legs twitching as he pressed his face against the cool glass. With all his being, he longed to be down there, doing what he loved best, kicking the ball against the wall, losing himself in the rhythm of it.

Kick, bounce, catch-ball-on-end-of-foot, kick, bounce . . .

When the game went well, his mind would click into neutral. His head would empty out, and his legs and arms would take over. The rhythm would satisfy and soothe him.

Jamal had flopped down onto his bed, stretching out his long, slender legs.

'Get away from the window,' he growled at Karim. 'They'll see you. They might take a pot shot.'

Karim turned his head and looked in the other direction. The Israeli tank that had been squatting at the crossroads just below the apartment block for days now had moved a few metres closer. A soldier was sitting on top of it, his gun

6

cradled in his arms. Beside the tank were three other men, one crouching down, talking into a mobile phone.

There was no chance, none at all, that he'd be able to go outside and play his game while the tank was there. Since a Palestinian gunman had shot two people in an Israeli café two weeks ago, the Israelis had set up another curfew, which meant that the whole city had been locked down. Everyone in Ramallah had been trapped indoors for those two weeks, unable to go out (except for a two-hour break once or twice a week) by night or day. If anyone tried – if they so much as stuck a foot out of their front door – the soldiers would open fire and blow it away. Jamal was right. Even standing by the window was dangerous.

He turned away. He wished now that he hadn't looked down at his football place. It had made him long to be outside, to be able to run and jump, to swing his arms and kick.

'Anyway,' he said to Jamal, 'I haven't noticed you being so fantastic at scoring yourself.'

Jamal turned his head to stare at him.

'What are you on about now?'

'You're a lousy shot. You know you are,' Karim said daringly. 'I saw you and your mates throwing stones at the tanks last week. You missed, every time. And don't pretend you weren't aiming properly, because you were.'

Jamal sat up and swung his legs over the side of the bed, pleased to have an excuse for a wrestling bout at last.

'You little spy. You've been following me again.'

He advanced on Karim, his arms outstretched. Karim shifted away, shuffling himself to the head of his bed, ruckling the scarlet blanket with his white-socked feet, his back against the wall, his hands held up in surrender.

'Lay off me, will you? I won't tell Mama. Not if you leave me alone.' He registered with satisfaction the look of caution that had crossed Jamal's face. 'And,' he went on, 'I won't tell

Baba either, if you give me one hour of totally unrestricted time on the computer without a single interruption. No, two.'

Disgusted, Jamal retreated. Karim could see that he was searching for something cutting to say, and failing. With one hunch of his shoulder, he turned away to the table, grabbed his headphones, hurled himself down onto his bed and clamped them to his ears.

Thrilled with his triumph, Karim jumped up and settled himself at the computer, which took up almost the whole of the table between the two beds. He would do it this time. He would get up to Level 5 in Lineman. He'd nearly managed it last week, but then there'd been a power cut and the computer had crashed just as victory was in sight.

He pushed the tottering pile of textbooks to the edge of the table. He had lists of English words to learn, as well as the dates of the Arab Conquests.

'They can stop you coming to school,' his teacher had said, before the curfew had been imposed, 'but don't let them stop you learning. Work at home. Your future is Palestine's. Your country needs you. Don't forget it.'

He'd tried to work once or twice, but it had been impossible to concentrate for long, with Jamal coming in and out of the room all the time, and Farah and Sireen, his two little sisters, noisily playing in the sitting room next door. After a few minutes, he'd usually ended up leafing through old comics and weaving delightful daydreams, imagining, for example, that Jamal was a million miles away, preferably in a space capsule endlessly orbiting round the planet Jupiter – or Saturn, he didn't mind which – and that the computer was his and his alone.

And now, for the next two hours, it was.

When my two hours are up I'll have a proper go at Biology, he told himself, as he stared at the screen, waiting for the game to boot up.

Peace settled on the room. Jamal had got up and gone back

into the sitting room, to settle himself on the old red velvet sofa and watch the news with his father. Sireen, who was four and had been crying all morning, had stopped at last, and Farah, who was eight, seemed to have gone across the landing to play with her best friend, Rasha, who lived in the apartment opposite.

The game began. At once, he was totally absorbed.

The opening moves were familiar. He'd played Lineman often enough to go through them almost automatically. Soon, though, he was doing the harder stuff. He tensed over the keyboard, his eyes boring into the screen, his fingers responding with lightning speed to his brain's commands. Slowly he was climbing through the levels. This time, he might really make it.

The door of the bedroom opened. He didn't look round, but he sensed his mother's presence. He needn't need to turn and look at her to know that a deep frown was scoring her forehead between her sharp black brows.

'You want an education, Karim, or you want to grow up like your uncle Bashir?' She paused, waiting for an answer. Karim said nothing. 'You want to mend roads for the next fifty years? Break your back in the hot sun, shovelling dirt?' Another silence. 'Suit yourself. Don't expect me to wash your dirty clothes for the rest of your life, that's all.'

He grunted, having barely heard what she had said. She sighed with exasperation and closed the door again. The game went on. One by one, the targets fell, and level succeeded level. Breathless, almost dizzy, Karim willed the screen to obey him, and when at last it exploded into stars as he reached the highest level, his head seemed to explode too.

'Ye-e-ess!' he yelled, and he slammed out of the bedroom into the sitting room and danced around the rest of his family, punching the air in triumph. 'I did it! I did it! Level Five! First time ever! Champion of the world! Victory is mine! Yield and obey, all lesser mortals!'

Jamal got up off the sofa.

'Level Five? In Lineman? Let's have a look.'

He pushed past Karim into the bedroom.

Hassan Aboudi, Karim's father, was sitting bent over on the sofa, staring at the TV screen, watching people wailing at a funeral. The announcer's solemn voice seemed to fill the room.

Five Palestinians, including two children, died during clashes between Israeli soldiers and stone-throwing youths in the West Bank town of Nablus this morning.

Hassan Aboudi turned to look angrily at Karim.

'Stop that noise at once,' he snapped. 'Get back to your homework or I'll take the damned computer away.'

Lamia, Karim's mother, was half reclining on an easy chair nearby. Her legs were crossed and a pink slipper dangled from her raised foot. Sireen had been sleeping against her chest, but she woke at the noise and struggled in her mother's arms, beginning to cry fretfully again. The mark of a button from Lamia's red blouse showed clearly on the little girl's cheek.

'Now look what you've done,' Lamia said reproachfully, lifting the damp black curls off Sireen's hot little forehead. 'You know how unwell she is. Don't you remember what earache feels like? I'd just got her settled, poor little thing. You might think what it's like for other people sometimes, Karim. Or is that really too much to ask?'

Jamal lounged back into the room, his hands in his pockets.

'It was only Level Four, you sad person. Thought you were one of the big boys, did you? Well, I've got news for you. You aren't.'

Karim felt his pleasure and triumph drain away and the miserable sense of imprisonment that the game had kept at bay for the last two happy hours closed in on him again.

10

'I hate you! You're lying! You know you are!' he shouted, aiming a blow at Jamal's chest.

Jamal laughed and ducked out of the way. Karim rushed back to look at the computer screen, but Jamal had turned the machine off. Now he couldn't prove a thing.

Desperate to be alone, to get away from his whole unbearable family, he went to the front door, opened it, stepped outside and closed it after him. The landing and stairs weren't much, but at least he'd be on his own for a bit.

Almost at once the door behind him opened again.

'Karim,' his father said, his voice tense with anxiety, 'what do you think you're doing? Get back in here at once.'

'I'm not going outside, Baba,' Karim said. 'I'll stay on the landing. I just – I need to be on my own for a bit.'

His father's face softened.

'All right, but only for a little while. Don't go near the window. Don't let them see you. Keep yourself out of sight. Come back in after ten minutes or your mother will start going crazy on me.'

The sound of the TV news followed Karim out through the open door of the flat.

Israeli troops shelled a refugee camp in Gaza this morning, killing nine Palestinians, including a three-year-old child. Five Israeli woman died and three children were badly injured when a Palestinian gunman opened fire in a crowded shopping street in Jerusalem this morning. A spokesman . . .

He pulled the door to behind him, shutting the voice out, then balled his fist and punched at the wall, painfully grazing his knuckles.